Sherlock Holmes and the devil's grail

'Watson,' Sherlock Holmes proclaimed, 'you know very well that it was one of those cases where I felt obliged to circumvent the law . . . I credit you with sufficient discretion not to expose me to a prosecution for murder . . .'

Thus the great detective discouraged Watson from publishing the story of the tobacco millionaire and the Glastonbury Fragment, one of the most bizarre investigations of their long partnership.

The curious persecution of Colonel Harden began in the spring of 1895. The Colonel, a hero of the Confederate States Army, millionaire tobacco planter and amateur archaeologist, had arrived in Britain with an ingenious stereoscopic camera of his own invention – a camera of great potential importance to criminal investigators and archaeologists.

The threats began the day he arrived – anonymous demands that he leave Britain – and they escalated to the abduction of the Colonel's son, Jay.

Behind it all Holmes discerned the hand of Drew, erstwhile lieutenant of the late Professor Moriarty, ex-Scotland Yard detective and blackmailer.

Drew and his gang feared that Colonel Harden might unearth a secret that they had sought since Moriarty's day, a priceless treasure that would give them power over the whole world.

The pursuit of the treasure and the unravelling of the secrets of a perverse religious cult brought Holmes, Watson and the Baker Street Irregulars to the haunted slopes of the Prescelly Mountains, where on a black Midsummer's Eve battle was joined and the forces of evil routed by the redoubtable detective and the devoted Doctor.

Also by Barrie Roberts

Sherlock Holmes and the railway maniac (1994)

SHERLOCK HOLMES
AND THE
DEVIL'S GRAIL

A Narrative believed to be from the pen of
John H. Watson, MD

Annotated and Edited for publication by
Barrie Roberts

This edition published in Great Britain in 2000 by
Allison & Busby Limited
114 New Cavendish Street
London W1M 7FD
http://www.allisonandbusby.ltd.uk

First published in Great Britain in 1995
by Constable & Company Ltd

A catalogue record for this book is available
from the British Library

ISBN 0 7490 0470 3

Set by Pure Tech Corporation, Pondicherry

Printed and bound by Biddles Limited,
Guildford, Surrey

Contents

Foreword

I have explained in another volume how a quantity of manuscripts which appear to be the work of John H. Watson came into my possession. In annotating and editing them for publication I have striven wherever possible to check their authenticity, despite the usual Watsonian mixture of real and fictitious names, but the evidence is not conclusive and, in the end, I must leave the question for the reader's decision.

Readers of *Sherlock Holmes and the Railway Maniac* should note that, while that purported to be Watson's record of Sherlock Holmes' last case, *The Devil's Grail* records a much earlier episode in the partnership.

The diagrams of the Glastonbury Fragment attached to Watson's manuscript were so badly faded as to be almost illegible and, for that reason, they have been redrawn.

Barrie Roberts, Walsall, September 1994

1

AN OLD ACQUAINTANCE

The many years of his practice as a consulting detective brought my friend Sherlock Holmes into contact with all manner of persons, from the most scurrilous villains to the highest in the land. In most cases he and I entered their lives briefly and dramatically and never saw nor heard of them again once the case was over. Only occasionally and incidentally did we learn what became of those who were not bound for the gaol or the gallows when we last saw them.

Holmes was singularly incurious about the fate of clients and witnesses. Once a case was completed his mind sought instantly for the stimulus of a fresh problem, and he reviewed old matters only in order to applaud or criticise his own methods. I, on the other hand, could not refrain from occasional speculation as to what had become of some of those we had met along the way.

It was, therefore, with the greatest pleasure that I dimly recognised the features of a well-dressed American gentleman who hailed me one night last winter outside the American Exchange in the Strand, though memory did not permit me to put a name to the face.

'Dr Watson!' he cried. 'It is Dr Watson, isn't it?' and he clasped my hand warmly.

My tongue fumbled for a name, and he laughed aloud at my embarrassment. 'No, sir! You would not recognise me. It's most of twenty-five years, and the last time you saw me I was a skinny youngster. My name is Harden, sir – John

Vincent Harden. When we first met I was John Vincent Harden junior!'

The name unleashed my recollections of one of the most grotesque cases in which Holmes and I were ever involved. In a very short time I had persuaded young Harden to join me in Simpson's over the best steak that London could offer in wartime, where we fell to reminiscing.

I call him 'young Harden' but he is now into his forties and good living has enlarged the slim youth I remembered. He shook his head in wonderment at the news that Holmes was now entirely devoted to his bee-keeping, and told me that his father, who had been our client so many years before, was now dead. Harden senior had made his millions in Virginia tobacco, but his son had expanded into other interests and was now in England on business connected with the supply of what he called 'canned goods' to the American Expeditionary Force in France.

'And you,' I asked, 'did you never pursue your theatrical interests?'

He smiled ruefully. 'No, doctor, Pa had his way and I became a tobacco-grower. My last and best performance was the one I gave for Mr Holmes. Still, it was a dandy part he gave me and the audience certainly went for it. I guess no theatre could have satisfied me after that! But my boy Jay, he's just as keen on the moving pictures as I was on the stage. He says when he's old enough he's off to California to make his name.'

He asked after the Baker Street Irregulars, that extraordinary band of street Arabs who were, for many years, the eyes and ears of Sherlock Holmes throughout the metropolis, and I had to tell him that two, to my certain knowledge, were dead in Flanders, but that another had received the Military Medal.

We passed a pleasant evening and separated on the pavement outside the restaurant, but the meeting caused me, at the next opportunity, to take out my notes of the Harden affair and relive the events of more than twenty years before. It seems to have had the same effect on him, for shortly afterwards I received a letter accompanied by a quantity of his family's tobacco. It does not, I have to say, smoke as well as the old Arcadia, but supplies of that mixture have become unreliable since the War and it is is a kind thought.

His letter is before me now:

Frenchman's Ridge,
Carran County,
Virginia,
USA.

22nd February 1918.

Dear Dr Watson,

Just a note to thank you again for your hospitality to a stranger on your shores last month. I enclose some of our product, which I hope will help you pass the time off duty and encourage you to remember a friend over here.

I'm only sorry that time did not permit me to call on Mr Holmes, but I guess from your account that he does not exactly welcome visitors anyhow. When you write him do give him my best regards and tell him I shall never forget the Glastonbury affair.

I sometimes wish that the whole story of that strange business might be told, so that Mr Holmes and you and my father might have your rightful credit for the parts you all played in it. Perhaps you will find it possible one day.

Yours,

John V. Harden.

I too would have wished to tell the story of the bizarre adventure which brought Holmes and the Harden family together, and I have more than once suggested to my friend that sufficient time has passed for it to be published. His response has always been the same. 'Watson,' he has said, 'you know very well that it was one of those

11

cases where I felt obliged to circumvent the law in more than one way. I may not admire your melodramatic accounts of my investigations, but I credit you with sufficient discretion not to expose me to a prosecution for murder, though I would deserve an acquittal. On the other hand, you cannot fairly tell the tale without admitting other actions of mine which would make me the subject of well-meant and completely misguided criticisms in the press. To be the subject of earnest moral debate in the columns of *The Times* is hardly conducive to a peaceful retirement'.

It is not for me to counter Holmes' wishes in the matter, but the case, as he himself has remarked, had certain interesting features and it cannot be so very long before neither he nor I can be bothered by any revelations. It is for those reasons, and in answer to young Harden's entreaty, that I have now set down the facts in the affair of the Devil's Grail, so that they may be published when Holmes and I are beyond harm or criticism. If John Vincent junior does not live to see it published, so be it, but I trust that his descendants may one day regain a unique piece of family history from this record, and the wider public may learn a little more of the curious skills of Sherlock Holmes.

2

AN IRRITATING OCCURRENCE

I have recorded elsewhere that the years immediately following my friend's return from his three years' exile were probably the busiest of his career, and the Harden case fell into that period. Nevertheless, a domestic tragedy in the family of our landlady had left us, for a few days in the spring of 1895, unavoidably idle. Mrs Hudson had been summoned to attend a death-bed in the North, together with her sister, Mrs Turner, who normally attended to our needs in the absence of Mrs Hudson. As a result Holmes and I found ourselves staying at an hotel during her absence.

Holmes was never at his best when not engaged in a case, and it was not long before he began to exhibit those symptoms of irritation that I knew so well. He had not, since his return from abroad, sought the consolations of his hypodermic syringe, but I was afraid that the continuing separation from his employment would drive him back to the use of cocaine. I tried, as ever, to distract him by suggesting various recreations, but his was not a recreative personality. His only real delight was in the exercise of his formidable intellectual processes upon some obscure problem, and life in a comfortable metropolitan hotel provided no stimuli for him. I began to hope, selfishly, that our landlady's kinsman might not linger on his death-bed.

We had returned to the hotel after a concert one evening when we were accosted in the lobby by a tall, fair-haired youth of some fifteen years. I recognised him as a fellow guest, having seen him in the hotel's dining-room with his parents and what I took to be two younger sisters. He addressed us in the long musical drawl that stems from the Southern United States.

'Please excuse me,' he said, 'but do I have the privilege of addressing Mr Sherlock Holmes and Dr Watson?'

'You do,' said Holmes, 'and may we know your identity?'

'I am John Vincent Harden junior,' said the youth, 'and I am staying here with my father and mother. I had seen you gentlemen coming and going and the clerk confirmed who you were. I just wished to say how much I admire your investigations, Mr Holmes. I have read all Dr Watson's accounts of your cases.'

Holmes smiled at the boy's enthusiasm. 'It is a pleasure to make your acquaintance, Mr Harden. If Dr Watson or I can be of any service to you or your family while you are in Britain, you know where to find us.'

The trace of a shadow seemed to pass across the boy's features. He paused a moment, then said, 'There is . . . there is no reason why we should trespass on your valuable time, Mr Holmes, but I thank you none the less. Please forgive my interrupting you,' and in a flash he had turned and stepped away across the lobby.

Holmes watched him go with a thoughtful expression, then turned to the counter clerk. 'What can you tell me about that young man?' he enquired, indicating the departing youth.

'Him, sir?' said the attendant, 'He's the son of Colonel Harden, the American tobacco millionaire. The whole family's been here a week. You must have seen them in the dining-room, sir – they always has the table in the bay window. Colonel Harden is a tall, dark gent, not unlike yourself, sir, and his wife is a pretty fair-haired lady. As well as the boy they've got two lovely little girls.'

'And what brings Colonel Harden and his family to London, do you know?' asked Holmes.

'Well, sir, we do get a lot of wealthy Americans come to London for pleasure these days,' said the clerk, as though the idea was extraordinary, 'but Colonel Harden is taking photographs of our historic buildings. It was in the papers yesterday.' He rummaged under his desk for a moment and produced a folded newspaper which he handed across. Holmes read the article quickly then passed it to me:

STEREOSCOPY AT THE TOWER OF LONDON

Visitors to the antiquities of our capital this week may have been surprised to come across an American gentleman accompanied by a mountain of photographic and scientific equipment. The gentleman has been seen for some days, at the Tower of London, St Paul's and other ancient buildings, apparently thrusting his lenses into the most unrewardingly dark corners of our celebrated landmarks.

This is not, as some may think, an unusually extreme form of the mania that grips our American cousins when they come face to face with buildings a good deal older than their Constitution, but a serious scientific enquiry being conducted by a gentleman of some note on the other side of the Atlantic.

Our visitor is none other than Colonel John V. Harden of Virginia, the millionaire owner of large tobacco interests in that state. Unlike certain other American 'Colonels' we have come across, he has a complete right to the rank, acquired during his service with the Army of the Confederacy in the unfortunate Civil War, a conflict in which he distinguished himself on more than one occasion.

Our correspondent caught up with the gallant and scientific gentleman at Westminster Abbey, where Colonel Harden was kind enough to explain his interest in our antiquities.

'The cameras I have brought with me', he explained, 'are of my own invention. They are a completely new

15

form of stereoscopic camera which, apart from producing the illusion of a three- dimensional image, enable the operator to deepen that image, so as to create an illusion that the distance between the objects recorded is greater than it is in actuality.'

He must have seen our correspondent's bewilderment, for he went on to explain that his instruments made it possible to record the least difference in a surface and to exaggerate that difference, so as to reveal details that would be invisible to the unassisted eye.

He had used his cameras to reveal inscriptions on the rock-dwellings of the Zuni Indians of New Mexico that had been scratched there by the Spanish Conquistadores, more than three centuries ago.

'I have brought my equipment to England to try it on some really ancient surfaces. I intend to see if I can seek out unknown inscriptions on your old cathedrals and your abbeys. I have made a fortune by serving one of mankind's trivial appetites, but I would like to be remembered for some more lasting contribution to the sum of human knowledge,' he told us.

Colonel Harden intends to continue his experiments on even older buildings when he leaves London, such as the prehistoric monuments at Stonehenge and Avebury and some of our ruined abbeys.

Holmes returned the newspaper to our informant, together with a small coin, and we made our way towards the stairs.

'I wonder,' Holmes mused as we prepared for bed, 'why the son of a millionaire who is also an amateur of archaeological photography should believe that his family might need my assistance, and why he should feel unable to mention the problem to me?'

On the following evening Holmes and I were a little late in our arrival at dinner. I was surprised to note that the Harden family, though all present, had abandoned the window table and were now occupying an alcove at the far side of the room. In the event my friend and I took advantage of the change to take the window table.

We had completed the main course and were lingering over our wine before taking dessert. Holmes' restlessness had been evident all day and was now taking the form of disjointed, sardonic remarks.

'Who was it, Watson, who remarked that relatives have not the least idea of how to live nor the smallest instinct about when to die?' he enquired, lifting his glass.

I was on the point of replying that I did not recognise the comment but I supposed he was applying it to our land-lady's family, when there came a sound like a hammer blow on the window behind Holmes and the entire pane shattered into fragments. Almost simultaneously the wine-glass that my friend had been holding exploded in his hand, spilling a tide of wine across the white table-cloth.

Nothing had touched me and I sprang to my feet. 'Holmes!' I cried. 'Are you all right?'

'I am unharmed, Watson,' he replied, shaking fragments of glass from his right hand on to the table, 'but this kind of thing is very irritating.'

3

A WARNING FROM HOLMES

Assured that my friend was not seriously injured, I ran from the dining-room and raced through the lobby to the hotel's front steps. As I reached their top I heard the crack of a whip and the rattle of wheels. From outside the hotel a closed carriage was tearing away down the street.

A solitary walker on the pavement lifted his cane and pointed towards the carriage, as though to confirm my view that the shot had been fired from within the vehicle. There were no cabs on the street and no policeman in sight. I could do nothing but return to Holmes.

The dining-room, when I returned to it, was in chaos. A number of diners, terrified by the attack on Holmes, had crowded out after me and some were already at the desk in the lobby, demanding their accounts. Others still sat at their tables, excitedly discussing the incident. Colonel Harden was shepherding his family up the stairs. Two waiters were already removing the debris from around the window table.

At first I could not see Holmes, then I realised that he was on his hands and knees in one corner of the room, intently searching the carpet under a table. Suddenly he sat back on his heels, holding something small between his thumb and forefinger.

'Ah!' he exclaimed. 'I thought so!' Catching sight of me, he hailed me. 'Ah, Watson! Have you lost your man?'

'I never had any chance of catching him,' I replied glumly as I walked over, and I outlined what I had seen in the street.

'No matter,' he consoled me. 'I have the missile, and that may well reveal something of the attacker.'

He pulled out a chair from an empty table and sat down, and I did likewise. The hotel's assistant manager had entered the dining-room and came across to us.

'Mr Holmes, doctor,' he said, 'I hope that neither of you is injured. Can I get you anything? A little brandy perhaps?'

'No, thank you,' said Holmes, raising a hand. 'We are both quite all right. I think not brandy; I dare say we are quite stimulated enough at present. Perhaps a half-bottle of the vintage that we had with dinner?'

While the wine was served I observed my friend. Despite his danger, the whole episode had refreshed him like water on a wilting plant. His colour was better and his eyes positively sparkled. He dropped a small object on to the tablecloth so that it rolled across the table to me.

'What do you make of that, Watson?'

I picked up a piece of steel, about half an inch long, cylindrical, with a diameter of about a quarter-inch. At one end it was filed to a point.

'It is some kind of home-made bullet,' I said. 'It has not been cast, it has been filed to shape and sawn from a piece of steel rod, I should think.'

'Precisely so,' said Holmes, 'and what manner of weapon uses such ammunition?'

'You would be hard put to it to fire that from any ordinary firearm,' I said. 'How would you enclose it in a cartridge?'

'Smell it!' commanded Holmes.

I sniffed at the missile, but could detect only a faint smell of the oil in which the steel rod would have been quenched.

'There is no smell of any explosive propellant,' I remarked.

'Exactly!' said Holmes. 'In other words, as you have already suggested, it was not propelled from a firearm.'

'An airgun?' I asked.

'So I should surmise,' said Holmes.

A thought crossed my mind. 'You surely do not think that Moriarty –' I began.

Holmes raised a hand to stop me. 'Moriarty, I do assure you, is dead, and it would be a serious error to assume that, just because he favoured airguns and his minions used them against me more than once, anyone who used an airgun against me was an agent of the late Professor.'

'But Holmes, it is scarcely a year since Moriarty's man Moran made an attempt on you with an airgun!'

'True, but the weapon that fired this,' he said, reaching for the bullet, 'was not crafted by von Herder, nor constructed in the Minories like Moriarty's weapons. This is most likely a missile from what is known as a "poacher's cane" or a "walking-stick gun".'

'I do not know the weapon.'

'There is no reason why you should, though had you practised medicine in the country you might have come across its effects. The poacher's cane is a simple but effective airgun, constructed of two metal cylinders which fit together in about the length and diameter of a country walking-stick. They contain a compression chamber and a firing mechanism. The pressure is pumped up by working one cylinder in and out of the other and, at full compression, the weapon can deliver a single powerful shot. They will accept a variety of commercial ammunition, but it is also possible to manufacture one's own, as you can see.'

'A walking-cane!' I exclaimed. 'The man on the street had such a cane!'

'Yes, Watson. He would have been the gunman. The carriage was there merely to distract attention if there was any serious pursuit. It is a slight pleasure to know that the attack was not launched by amateurs.'

'But who would attack you at this time, Holmes?' I asked.

Holmes gave a short laugh. 'Good heavens, Watson! That shot was neither aimed at me nor intended for me!

Now, let us finish our wine. We have a witness to interview if he will co-operate.'

As we left the dining-room Holmes asked the assistant manager if he knew where Colonel Harden might be found.

'I believe he took his family to their rooms after the attack on you, Mr Holmes, and I have not seen him since.'

'I wonder,' asked Holmes, 'if you would be good enough to take him my card and ask him if he will do us the honour of waiting on us in the smoking-room?'

The incident in the dining-room had driven many guests to their rooms or to the bar, so that the smoking-room was empty when we entered. We lit cigars and, in a short time, the American Colonel joined us. He was a tall, lean man in his sixties. His dark hair was greying and he wore long side-whiskers. His erect carriage betrayed his military past.

'Mr Holmes, doctor,' he said, 'as I think you know, I have the honour to be Colonel John V. Harden. I hope that neither of you is any the worse for that frightening incident at dinner?'

We assured him that we were unscathed and Holmes offered the Colonel a cigar. When it was alight and our guest was seated, he looked at both of us.

'You asked me to call on you, Mr Holmes. Is there some way I can be of assistance to you?'

Holmes blew smoke into the air. 'I had hoped, Colonel Harden, that you would be able to tell us in what way we may be of assistance to you,' he said, quietly.

Harden stiffened. 'I don't believe I understand you. I am sorry for the attack on you. I had hoped that London would be a deal more law-abiding than some shanty town on the Blue Ridge, and I will help you in any way that I can to lay the villains by the heels, but I don't see how you figure that I need your help!'

Holmes smiled. 'Colonel Harden, last night Dr Watson and I made the acquaintance of your son, an admirable young man. He came within an ace of telling us that there

21

was some way that we could assist his family, but his nerve failed him at the last moment.'

The American had started forward in his chair, but Holmes raised a hand to forestall him. 'Hear me out, please, Colonel! This evening you and your family abandoned your usual table in the bay window and ate at the other end of the room. In the course of the meal a shot was fired from the pavement that almost struck the person sitting in your usual place, a person who is of the same build and colouring as yourself. It is impossible to resist the inference that you are under some kind of threat and had forewarning of the impending attack.'

'Mr Holmes,' said our guest, 'you disappoint me. I have read so much of your wonderful powers of deduction, but you've read this one all wrong. I can only imagine that your narrow escape from danger has diverted your thoughts.'

'You do us both less than justice, Colonel. You, of all people, know that there was no danger. I am sure that you are an honourable man and, had you believed for one moment that the person who took your place was in real danger, you would have occupied the seat yourself at whatever risk. You believed that no action would be taken against a stranger seated in the window, and overlooked the possibility that the stranger might resemble you. No – you knew full well that that shot was a warning. If the gunman had wished to harm the person sitting in your chair, he had every opportunity to do so. It was a clear warning, Colonel Harden, and you may save yourself much mischief if you tell us what it meant.'

Harden stood up. 'I'm sorry, gentlemen,' he said, 'I can only repeat that you appear to have hold of the wrong end of this affair, Mr Holmes. I have no enemy in Britain – indeed, I never set foot in your country until days ago. My family and I are not in any danger and I cannot help you further. I wish you both good-night.'

'Very well,' said Holmes, 'if that is the way you propose to treat the matter; but if you will not be warned by your enemies, be warned by a disinterested bystander – the attack tonight showed every sign of organisation and cunning. I do not withdraw my offer of assistance. You may reject the offer now, but the time will come when you will ask for my help. Good-night to you, Colonel.'

Harden strode from the room without another word.

4

AN URGENT SUMMONS

By the time we breakfasted next day, Colonel Harden and his family had already set out on their day's business, and shortly afterwards we received news that Mrs Hudson was back at Baker Street and waiting to welcome us.

We lost no time in packing our bags and paying our bill, so that by mid-morning we were cheerfully re-established in our old quarters. No sooner had we arrived than Holmes flung himself on to the couch and began to stare at the wall while he rolled the steel bullet in his fingers and mused on the threat against the Hardens.

After a few hours of his silent meditation, I ventured to suggest that he had, in his own terms, insufficient data to form any reasonable theory.

'Watson,' he said, 'I have told you before that the resources of the human brain are infinite and largely unknown to us. There are philosophers in the Orient who believe that all things are entirely indicative of their time and that a proper understanding of any one thing will reveal all that can be known of its time and the events surrounding it. One of our earliest arguments arose because I offered you the proposition that it is theoretically possible to infer the existence of an ocean from a grain of sand. Why should not this bullet be capable of impeaching the man that fired it?'

I abandoned the conversation and turned to my books. Holmes was still meditating on the bullet when, late in the evening, Mrs Hudson informed us that we had a caller.

When Holmes knew that it was not a message from the Colonel he was less than anxious to deal with the matter. I told him that our visitor was a handsome young woman (for I had seen her crossing the street to our lodgings), but he was obdurate.

'Watson!' he cried. 'I do not share your predilection for the fair sex. I regard them as a snare and a distraction. Tell the young lady that it is Saint George's Day and that I keep it as my national holiday – tell her I have gone to Stratford upon Avon to celebrate Shakespeare's birthday – tell her what you will, Watson, but send her away!'

'Holmes,' I grumbled, 'it seems to me that you have departed from your own logical outlook! On the one hand you have passed most of today in attempting to unravel the problems of Colonel Harden, who would not, it seems, thank you for the solution if you handed it to him on a plate! On the other hand is this poor young woman, who has travelled heaven knows how far to lay her problem before you – and she I must send away!'

He sat up and stared at me without expression for several seconds. 'Very well, Watson,' he said at last, 'if it will make you any easier I will see the young woman. Have her shown in and let us see if we can dispose of her problem,' and he swung his long legs to the floor.

Despite his sardonic comments on her sex, once our visitor had been shown in Holmes was the soul of courtesy, and within minutes Miss Violet Smith was outlining to us the events which I have already narrated under the title of 'The Solitary Cyclist'.

Holmes was not uninterested in Miss Smith's problem, but was not to be budged from Baker Street. After she had gone he announced that I should travel to Surrey early on Monday to carry out certain investigations in the matter.

'I, Holmes?' I queried. 'Surely it would be better all round if you were to visit Surrey? I never seem to approach these things in the way you consider appropriate. We may save a deal of wasted effort if you are first on the ground.'

'Watson, those who threaten Colonel Harden are professionals – they are both cunning and bold. At any moment they may move to a more dangerous degree of action. When that occurs, I wish to be available. You go to Surrey, Watson. I know you will do your best.'

In the event, my best endeavours in Surrey were so inadequate in Holmes' opinion that, on the following afternoon, he ventured there himself. I would have been less than human if I had not found a certain satisfaction at seeing him return with a bruised forehead and a cut lip, though he was in high good humour, having sent his opponent home in a cart.

A week after Miss Smith's call we were both in Surrey and, by the end of that day, we had returned to Baker Street with a satisfactory conclusion to the young lady's problem. Holmes turned his mind once more to Colonel Harden's strange behaviour. By noon the next day our sitting-room was thick with the smoke of his pipe, as he sat like some Buddha on a pile of cushions.

'Could it be his war service?' he asked, after a silence that had lasted two hours.

'Whose? Harden's?' I queried. 'The American Civil War was thirty years ago, Holmes. Surely any old scores from that conflict are long settled.'

'Maybe . . . maybe . . . though there are still those who seek the missing Confederate Treasury gold. Then again, the murderers of Lincoln were never brought to justice.'

'Surely Booth was shot and his fellow conspirators hanged?' I said.

'Small fry,' said Holmes, waving a dismissive hand. 'The organising genius behind the plot was never caught.'

'Are you suggesting that Harden is connected with the theft of the Confederate Treasury or the murder of Abraham Lincoln?' I asked.

'Not really,' said Holmes. 'I was merely indicating that Colonel Harden's war, like all wars, left unfinished business behind it, and no war is more productive of rancour than a civil war.'

'I would have thought,' I said, 'that the answer lies in his wealth. Surely he has given real or imagined offence to someone in his business dealings and now they seek revenge.'

'Very good, Watson, very good – but why in England? The Colonel has never set foot here before. Surely such a vendetta would be localised to Virginia, or at least the United States?'

I had not framed a reply when a tap at the door heralded Mrs Hudson. She offered Holmes a visitor's card which brought a wide smile to his features before he passed it to me. The ornately engraved card bore the American eagle and the words 'Laurence G. Crane, Embassy of the United States of America'.

Holmes chuckled gleefully. 'I fancy that this indicates a development in our plot, Watson! Do please show the gentleman in, Mrs Hudson, and bring us some tea.'

A stocky, fresh-complexioned young man was ushered in and I offered him the basket chair. He was clad in the sober dress of the diplomatic service and he looked around him, wide-eyed, at our unconventional sitting-room.

'Mr Crane,' said Holmes, 'I am Sherlock Holmes and this is my friend and partner Dr Watson. What has happened to Colonel Harden?'

The young man started. 'Colonel Harden, sir? Why do you say that something has happened to him? I have mentioned it to nobody!'

'It is a part of my business to know things that I have not been told, Mr Crane. Now, take your tea and tell us what brings you here.'

'I have an urgent message for you, sir. It is from Colonel Harden. The Ambassador has had a wire from the Colonel and I was ordered to bring it straight here and attend you on your journey.'

'A journey, eh?' said Holmes, and rubbed his hands. 'Things are getting better and better, Watson! And where might we be going, Mr Crane?'

The American reached inside his hat and extracted a slip of paper. 'Perhaps you had better see Colonel Harden's message, sir.' Holmes read the message then passed it to me. It was on a sheet of unheaded stationery, scrawled in rapid pencil:

> Contact Holmes, 221b Baker Street, with Colonel John V. Harden's apologies and request for most urgent assistance. Special waiting at Waterloo. Rooms booked at White Swan, Winchester, for Holmes and assistant. Expense no object. Cannot exaggerate urgency.
>
> John V. Harden, CSA (Retd)

'That is as much as the Embassy knows, Mr Holmes,' said Crane. 'It arrived by messenger from Winchester less than an hour past and I was told off to attend you and get you to Winchester.'

'And if I was not willing to go?' asked Holmes.

'His Excellency gave me *carte blanche* to get you to Winchester by any means necessary, sir. He is a particular friend of Colonel Harden's.'

'Then we will not try Anglo-American relations, nor embarrass you, Mr Crane. If you will give my colleague and me time to pack we shall accompany you to Waterloo. Though Colonel Harden was neither frank nor friendly with me last time we met, I sense that his attitude has softened.'

Inside an hour we were rattling south-west out of Waterloo in a first-class carriage coupled to a fast engine. Our sudden departure had deprived us of luncheon, but a well-stocked hamper had been put aboard. Holmes, who would go for days without food when his deductive processes were blocked, applied himself cheerfully to the food and wine.

'Tuck in, Watson!' he said. 'Tuck in! You should remember your soldiering days and take refreshment where you find the chance. After all, if Colonel Harden is not prepared to be fully frank with me when we meet, we may well find ourselves walking back to Baker Street!'

THE PERSECUTION
OF COLONEL HARDEN

'Let me say right away, Mr Holmes, that I owe you an apology for the way I treated you in London. Not only did I expose you and Dr Watson to danger, but I as good as called you a liar when you told me I needed assistance. Well, sir, I do need that assistance now, though I would understand if you were to refuse me.'

The man who met us in Winchester was a very different Colonel Harden from the proud American we had seen in London. Now his whole figure was stooped and his lean face was pale and strained. Upon our arrival he had ushered his red-eyed wife and daughters into another room, then turned to make his apology to Holmes.

My friend waved a hand dismissively. 'All that is past, Colonel. No doubt you believed you acted for the best. Even I am not free from error. I will, of course, assist you, provided that you answer my questions fully and frankly.'

'Of course, sir,' said the Colonel.

'Then why have you summoned me with such urgency?'

A bitter spasm passed across the American's features. 'My son Jay – John Vincent junior – has disappeared! He has been taken by the scoundrels who have threatened me!'

'You had best,' said Holmes, dropping uninvited into an armchair, 'begin at the beginning. Who is threatening you and when did it start?'

'That's the devil of it, Mr Holmes! I do not know who threatens me!' cried the Colonel. 'But it began the moment

I set foot in your country and it has gone on ever since, growing more ominous on each occasion!'

'Tell me!' commanded Holmes.

'The very day we landed – as I stood on the quayside – a stranger standing behind me said, "Colonel Harden, you would be wise to return to America with your ship." I could scarcely believe my ears. I looked all around, but I saw nobody who seemed to have spoken that message.'

'And then?'

'In the unshipping of our baggage, one of my wife's trunks was lost. It was found by the shipping company and delivered to our hotel on the next day. It had been locked, sir – securely locked – but when it was opened it contained an envelope addressed to me. It was a threat in the same terms – to leave England immediately.'

'Do you have the note?' asked Holmes.

'I destroyed it. I did not wish my family to know of the threats.'

'A pity,' said Holmes. 'No matter. What was next?'

'I came to England to carry out certain photographic experiments. I am the inventor of –'

'An extremely ingenious camera that will be of great assistance to the criminal investigator as well as the archaeologist, Colonel,' Holmes interrupted. 'I have read your explanations in the press and look forward to making the acquaintance of your device. You pressed on with your experiments?'

'Indeed, sir. I believed that the messages were mere nonsense, issued by some lunatic Socialistic or Anarchistic group because I was known to be wealthy. Then I was threatened again at Westminster Abbey.'

'In the abbey itself!' I said, shocked.

'Yes, doctor. I had set up my camera and had my head under the camera-cloth, making the final adjustments, when a voice spoke right beside me. It said, "Colonel Harden, you would be wise to take our advice and go home by the next boat!" '

'What did you do?' asked Holmes.

'I wrenched the cloth from my head, but whoever spoke must have moved like lightning. There was no one in my vicinity.'

'And next?'

'At every place I set up my apparatus I would receive a threat – always quietly spoken by people who must have been nearby. Then I had another written message.'

'What sort of voices made the threats? Were they male? Young? Educated? Had they any accents?'

'It was a peculiar voice, sort of high-pitched and husky at the same time. As far as I could distinguish it was the voice of a man in middle age, but I am not very familiar with British accents.'

'What did the written message say?'

'Something to the effect that I made myself an easy target by sitting in the hotel's window and that if I didn't go home they would show me how easy.'

'And we know what followed from that,' said Holmes. 'Has anything else occurred since you left London?'

'No, Mr Holmes, nothing – nothing until the vermin took my boy!' Harden's face contorted with a mixture of rage and grief.

'Calm yourself, Colonel,' said Holmes. 'I have every confidence that your son will come to no harm. Tell me how he fell into their hands.'

'Yesterday,' said the Colonel, making a visible effort to control his emotions, 'yesterday Jay went out in the afternoon to visit a store around the block – a little place that sells candy and cigars. He was gone a long while, so long that I took a stroll round there myself. I saw no sign of him, but I did see that the shop was almost opposite the theatre.'

'Is that significant?' I asked.

'Jay cannot pass by a playhouse, doctor,' said Harden. 'He simply dotes on actors and actresses. I had thought he might have gone in there until I spoke to the storekeeper.'

'What did he say?' asked Holmes.

'He remembered Jay. He said the boy had bought candy then gone across to look at the bills outside the theatre. He had seen him standing outside, by the alley to the stage door, talking to two men.'

Holmes' eyes brightened. 'Can he describe these men?'

'He took little notice of them, but he says that one was a large, heavily built man and the other somewhat slighter. Both had light overcoats and hats.'

'What transpired between them and your son?'

'We don't know. The cigar-store man said that he looked across the street a couple of minutes later and they were gone.'

'Has the alley been examined?' asked Holmes.

'I went straight there. It leads only to the stage door of the theatre, and that was locked from inside, but there is a gap in the fence of the alley which would allow someone to slip on to the waste lot behind the theatre. I found this in the alley,' said the Colonel, and drew a small paper packet from his pocket.

He placed it on the table and Holmes picked it up and examined it. It was a conical twist of cheap white paper, containing a handful of sweets. Holmes turned it in his long fingers and sniffed at it. 'Pear drops,' he noted to himself before looking up at the American.

'What,' he said, 'do you believe has happened to your son?'

'He was lured into the alley by some promise of getting inside the theatre. Once in the alley they drugged him or sapped him and dragged him through that hole in the fence, on to the waste lot. I guess they had a carriage there.'

'Precisely,' said Holmes. 'What lies beyond the waste ground?'

'The roads north out of the city, the main railway station –' I began, but Harden interrupted me.

'You see, Mr Holmes? They could have had him on a train in minutes! He may be in London, or anywhere in Britain – he might even be on the Continent!'

'This is rootless speculation,' said Holmes, rising. 'We need more data. Have you informed the county police?'

'As soon as I realised the boy was missing.'

'And what is their theory?'

'That Jay has been taken for ransom. The police chief says I may expect to hear from the villains soon.'

'He must watch more melodramas than your son,' said Holmes. 'This is not a matter of ransom, Colonel. Such abductions are as unknown in Britain as they are in your country. What is more, ransomers would have communicated with you as fast as possible, if only to try and prevent you setting the police on their trail.'

'Charlie Ross was taken from his parents' lawn in Philadelphia,' said the Colonel, 'and never found.'

'The exception that proves the rule,' said Holmes. 'An incident so unique that it outraged the United States. Besides, in the Ross case there was an extensive series of ransom demands. No, Colonel, abduction for ransom belongs to the Mediterranean and southern Europe, not to Winchester. We have something else here.'

He turned to the door. 'Let us go and examine the ground,' he said, 'after which I believe I may offer you some inferences.'

It was but a few minutes' walk to the street by the theatre. Holmes visited the tobacconist and questioned him, but he could add nothing to the account he had given Colonel Harden and the police. We crossed to the alley beside the theatre and Holmes spread his arms at the entrance, to prevent the Colonel or me from entering before him.

As we waited at the entry, Holmes paced cautiously along the middle of the passageway, his eyes fixed on the ground. From time to time he would touch or probe the dirt with the tip of his stick. Once he stooped and teased something out of the yellowed grass that crept under the boarding.

At the far end he took out his pocket lens and examined the boards around the gap in the fence, plucking something from them, then signalled to us to follow and stepped through the gap. We caught up with him on the waste plot alongside the theatre. It was the usual patch of dirt and brick rubble left by the removal of a building and the spring sunshine had baked its surface hard.

'No footprints here, Holmes,' I ventured.

'No,' he replied, thoughtfully, 'but there may yet be valuable indications. Wait here a moment.'

He paced backwards and forwards across the patch of dirt in a careful pattern, his eyes always on the ground, and here and there he stooped again. After some fifteen minutes he returned to us.

'There is no more to be learned here,' he said. 'Let us return to the hotel, where I can give you my conclusions.'

Back in the Hardens' suite Holmes took up a position before the window. The Colonel and I sat and looked to him expectantly.

'Now, Colonel Harden, we have some information and it is possible to draw certain inferences,' announced Holmes. 'Firstly, and most importantly, your son has not come to any serious harm.'

'How can you say so?' demanded Harden.

'Precisely because he was not taken for ransom,' Holmes replied. 'In such a case the object is to lay hands on the money and the fate of the victim is secondary. Little Charlie Ross is, I am sure, long since dead. Here we are dealing with skilful professionals, who have already shown that they are reluctant to kill, even when they can do so with impunity. If, on the other hand, they had wished to kill the boy, they had only to slit his throat in that alley and vanish without any useful trace.'

The American shuddered at Holmes' expression. 'You make a good deal of sense,' he said, 'but if it isn't murder and it isn't ransom, what in tarnation is this all about?'

'Your boy is being held as a warning, or perhaps as a hostage. Whoever may be your persecutors, one thing is clear – they are earnestly intent on you leaving England. They have given you spoken and written warnings which you have ignored; they have threatened your own safety without impressing you. Now they seek to weaken your resolve by an attack on your family.'

'But why Jay and not my wife or one of the girls?'

Holmes chuckled drily. 'Your son's devotion to the stage made him the more vulnerable member of the family. We

34

know that you have been closely watched since your arrival in Britain. They would easily see that your son regularly used the sweetshop opposite the theatre, rather than the nearer shop which we passed on the way there, and that he always paused to read the playbills. Easy enough to lie in wait and lure him into a trap.'

'What do you believe happened, Holmes?' I asked.

'Those who have kept watch on the family saw Jay leave the hotel. They waited in the alley's mouth while he went to the sweetshop, where one of them dropped his cigarette end. Having engaged the boy in conversation they drew him into the alley under some pretext, where he was overcome by this,' and he drew a piece of cloth from his coat pocket and flung it into my lap.

It was a torn piece of cotton sheeting and I did not need to pick it up to catch its familiar odour.

'Chloroform!' I exclaimed.

'Indeed,' said Holmes. 'Once senseless, your son was manhandled through the fence and loaded into a waiting carriage, a four-wheeler probably driven by a third associate who had smoked two cheap black cheroots while he waited. In the process of loading, a metal button came off the boy's grey flannel jacket and he dropped the pear drop which he had been sucking. With at least four persons on board, the carriage was sufficiently weighty to leave some slight traces on the ground. It left the waste ground in a northerly direction.'

The Colonel had listened wide-eyed to this detailed narrative. 'The jacket! The button!' he ejaculated. 'How did you know?'

'Elementary, my dear Colonel,' said Holmes. 'The boards bore a wisp of light grey wool, which we know was not from the villains' clothing, and the button lay beside the carriage's wheel-marks.' He drew it from his pocket and laid it on the table. 'I think you can distinguish the inscription of the American Button Corporation of New York on the obverse.'

'Marvellous!' said Colonel Harden, and picking up the button turned it over and over in his hands. 'You are every bit as astute as the doctor has said.'

'I am merely practised in the arts of observation and deduction, Colonel, but they will not, alas, help me to answer your next question.'

Harden looked up. 'You mean – where have they taken him?'

Holmes nodded. 'I can tell you where they have not taken him,' he said. 'He is not in London, nor abroad. To carry a senseless youth of your son's size into a railway station would be bound to attract attention, as it would at a port. Besides, the nearest port is some twenty miles distant. They would not care to travel that far unless it was absolutely necessary. I imagine that they have a headquarters within ten miles of this city.'

'Then the police can search,' said Harden. 'People will have seen the carriage . . .'

Holmes raised a hand. 'There are literally hundreds of remote cottages, farms and even mansions in the hills around Winchester – far too many for even the entire county force to search. In addition, private carriages leaving the city are commonplace. There is nothing so invisible as the ordinary.'

'Then what can we do?' asked the Colonel.

'I believe that your son's abductors intend you to spend a while imagining all that might have happened to the boy. When they judge that the time is ripe they will contact you and make a further demand that you leave the country as a condition of the lad's return. When they do so we may have the chance to learn who and where they are and what is at the bottom of this singular business.'

Colonel Harden smote the arm of his chair with frustration. 'By damn, Mr Holmes, this is hard! Surely there is something we can do?'

'I suggest,' said Holmes, 'that we take a little refreshment, while we discuss what may lie at the back of this series of incidents. We may, unknowingly, possess sufficient information to point towards the perpetrators.'

6

JAY HARDEN'S NARRATIVE

Holmes leaned forward over the tea table and steepled his two hands in front of his face.

'Now, gentlemen,' he said, 'we must consider what we may know that bears on the motive of young Jay's abductors. Why should a gang of apparently skilled professional criminals be so engaged by Colonel Harden's photographic activities?'

The Colonel started. 'You think that?' he asked. 'You believe my stereoscope is behind it?'

'I begin there,' said my friend, 'because I see no other possible starting point. Something about your presence here is seen by someone as a threat. Now, the only thing that is the least bit unusual about the presence of a wealthy American family in Britain is your photographic experiments, therefore I suggest a possible connection.'

The Colonel looked bewildered.

'A rival?' I ventured. 'Someone who fears your process for commercial reasons and wishes to suppress it?'

Harden shook his head slowly. 'I should not have thought so,' he said. 'I know some men will give a business rival a pretty rough ride, but not this. They say Edison is pretty tough on people, but he's not interested in the stereoscope any more. Sure, he makes them, but he says moving pictures will be a bigger thing.'

'Has anyone made an offer for your idea?' asked Holmes.

'No,' said the Colonel, 'and if they did I couldn't take it. It's an experimental camera, it's not ready to market. Too many of the adjustments can't be measured and have to be made by guess and by instinct. It needs all sorts of refinements yet. Besides, there are no valuable patents in stereoscopy. Your Wheatstone laid down the principle before photography was invented; my camera only refines his theory.'

'Then the reasons are unlikely to be commercial,' said Holmes, 'and if they were they would have been pursued in America. It seems to me that your persecutors merely wish to halt your experiments, and that suggests that they believe your activities may harm them in some way.'

'I cannot see any harm to anyone in my photographs,' said Harden. 'When they don't work I've wasted my own time and money, and when they do I've added a little more to our knowledge of ancient buildings. What possible harm is there in that?'

'An insane archaeologist?' I hazarded. 'Some monomaniac academic whose theories may be destroyed by your camera?'

Holmes laughed shortly. 'I grant you,' he said, 'that there are no more dangerous animals than academics when their cherished beliefs are threatened, but their weapons are the heavily sarcastic review, the poisonous paper and the public lecture. I should be most surprised if they took to unusual airguns and the taking of hostages. Besides, until the Colonel makes public a result, they could have no idea of any discovery he might make.'

A tap at the door heralded one of the hotel's staff, who apologised for intruding but said there was a messenger downstairs with a message for the Colonel.

Harden's face brightened. 'Send him up, man! Send him up!'

'I hesitated to do so, sir, because of the nature of the messenger, sir. It is a boy, sir – a distinctly dirty farm boy. He has been asked to deliver his message and go, sir, but he insists on seeing you personally.'

'Then bring him in, dirt and all!' commanded the Colonel and the manager left hurriedly. Harden turned back

38

to us. 'You were right, Mr Holmes. They have waited a while and now they've sent us a messenger.'

Within moments the manager returned, ushering before him a youth clad in the greasiest suit of corduroys I have ever seen. A filthy rag of neckcloth was wound about his collar and his feet were encased in muck-spattered gaiters and broken-toed boots. His face, deeply engrained with dirt, was partly concealed by an oversized cap, pulled well down.

He stood, two paces from the table, hands thrust in either pocket, and peered at each of us in turn.

'You're Sherlock 'Olmes,' he announced to my friend, in a ripe Hampshire burr, 'an' you're Dr Watson.'

Both of us nodded in acknowledgement, but the manager was outraged. 'Take your hands from your pockets and take off your hat, boy!' he snarled, and grabbed the youth's cap from his head.

Holmes shouted with laughter and Colonel Harden's eyes started as the removal of the greasy urchin's cap revealed the long fair locks of John Vincent Harden junior.

In a moment the Colonel was embracing his son with tears in his eyes, Holmes was pacifying the confused manager with a coin and the Colonel's wife and daughters were pouring into the room at the sound of Harden's cries of joy.

Over the scenes of family rejoicing let me draw a veil. Suffice it to say that it was an hour later that Holmes, Colonel Harden and I sat down with a much cleansed and partly refreshed Harden junior to hear his account of his adventures.

He told us how he had been accosted outside the theatre and described the two men. 'The one who spoke,' he said, 'was fatter than the other and bigger. I didn't pay much mind to the little fellow, he was kind of pale-faced and thin, but the bigger fellow had a round, pink face and a fat nose. He looked a bit like a pig and he sounded funny.'

'How did he speak?' asked Holmes. 'You have a good ear for accents, young man; tell us how he spoke.'

The boy screwed up his face in concentration, then repeated the words that the larger man had said to him: 'Good afternoon, sonny. I see that you are interested in the theatre.'

Holmes listened carefully, then turned an interrogative expression to me.

'A diseased larynx,' I said, surprised at the perfection with which the boy had reproduced the symptoms.

'Very probably,' said my friend, and waved his right hand as though conducting an orchestra. 'Again!' he commanded.

As the phrase was repeated Holmes closed his eyes and threw back his head. At the end his eyes snapped open. 'That is Drew!' he said. 'There is no doubt about it, that is Drew's voice!' He turned to the Colonel. 'Your son has the most acute ear,' he said. 'His record is more faithful than the phonograph.'

'I think that is one of the voices that have threatened me,' said the American, in a bewildered tone, 'but who is this Drew?'

'Drew,' said Holmes, 'is a gentleman of unsavoury antecedents who came close to being locked up four years ago. When I dealt with his master I left the evidence to convict Drew and his cronies a dozen times over, but my friends at Scotland Yard tell me that he escaped because highly prized reputations might have been besmirched had he stood trial and witnesses became unwilling. It will be a particular pleasure to foil any enterprise of his.'

He flourished a commanding hand at the boy. 'Pray continue with your narrative,' he said.

Young Harden continued, confirming Holmes' deductions as to the manner of his being taken away. He had recovered from the effects of the chloroform to find himself sprawled on the seat of a closed carriage, and had the wit to conceal his recovery from the two bandits who sat opposite him.

He had, of course, no means of knowing where he was until the carriage swung left off the road.

'I felt it running over a long, very bumpy track that curved around to the right, then we halted. The two men in the carriage called the driver for help, and the three of them dragged me out. I just went on playing possum and they slung me between the three of them and carried me into a big house.'

'What manner of house?' said Holmes. 'Did you see?'

'Oh, I saw it all right. It was big, like a plantation house, with a big porch and pillars. I remember thinking that I didn't know there were houses like that in England. Then I saw the front of the house was covered in creeper. It looked thick, like it hadn't been trimmed for quite a while.'

'Aha!' exclaimed Holmes. 'A bumpy, unweeded drive, a pillared portico and unkempt creeper on the frontage. It is only the beginning of May. To be significantly untrimmed that creeper must grow on a house that has been untenanted for over a year. We are accumulating facts, gentlemen, and we shall soon be able to identify the house. What was the interior like, young man?'

'I caught a glimpse of the hallway as they carried me through. It was wide, with two staircases curving up. There was no carpet in the hall or on the stairs, and their boots echoed on the floor. I guess the house was mainly empty.'

'Where did they take you?' asked Holmes.

'We went up the left-hand stair and along some passages. They echoed too, so I guess there was no furniture there. Then we went up a little staircase at the back of the house, right up to the top. There were a couple of little rooms at the top and they took me into one and just dropped me on a bed.'

'Was the bed made up?'

'No, sir. It was just an iron bedstead with slats across. I still played dumb, so they locked me in. A few minutes later the driver came back and dropped a pile of blankets on the bed, then he locked me in again.'

'Had they spoken while they carried you up?' enquired Holmes.

'They said that I had to be put away quickly, as the less that knew I was there the better. That scared me badly. I thought they were going to do away with me.'

'What did you do when they left you locked in?'

'I sat up and started looking for a way out. I didn't intend to stay around if I could help it, but there didn't seem to be a way. The door was solid and locked on the other side. There was only one little window and I looked out and could see I was three floors up with a sheer wall outside. Anyhow, the window was nailed shut.'

'So how did you escape?' I asked.

'Don't interrupt the boy, Watson! How did you manage to escape?' asked Holmes.

'I thought I was stuck, but then I saw a hatchway in the ceiling. I guessed it had to lead somewhere, so I tried to reach it, but it was too high. I climbed on the head of the bed, but I still couldn't reach the edge of the hatch. Then I heard the key in the lock, so I lay down and played sleepy.'

'Who was it?'

'It was the driver again. He had a plate of sandwiches and a jug of cider. He didn't say anything, he just put them on the floor and went. I was getting powerful hungry by this time, so I took some food, though I was a bit afraid they might have poisoned it. After that I felt better and I could think a bit better. I thought that if I up-ended the bedstead I could use it like a ladder to get to the hatch, but I was worried about the noise it would make. I couldn't figure out how to do it without a sound. I spent a lot of time on that one, but I couldn't crack it. Then I heard this really strange noise down in the house.'

'What kind of noise?' said Holmes.

'It was weird, some kind of chanting or something, with drums banging and shouts. I'd never heard anything like it, except perhaps . . .' He paused as though confused.

'Except when?' said Holmes, encouragingly.

'In New Orleans – on Congo Square where the voodoo drummers dance. The noise in that house sounded the same.'

'When were you on Congo Square?' the Colonel demanded angrily.

'When I visited with Aunt Mimi she took me there. She said it was a sight everyone should see, and it was pretty exciting, all the black folk dancing and drumming and chanting under the flares.'

'Your Aunt Mimi must be crazy!' snorted the Colonel. 'A young boy and a white woman on Congo Square at night!'

'We was alright, Pa,' said Jay. 'A friend of Aunt Mimi's escorted us – Mr Bolden. He's a musician with his own orchestra.'

'I shall have words with your aunt next time I'm in New Orleans!' said the Colonel. 'He can't be right, Mr Holmes. Congo Square is voodoo and mumbo-jumbo from Africa.'

'He may be more right than we know,' said Holmes. 'So you took advantage of the noise to risk moving the bed-stead?'

'Yes, sir. After that it was no trouble to scramble up through the hatch. It led to a sort of loft, full of all kinds of rubbish. It was pretty dark but it was at the top of the house and there was a bit of light coming up through the eaves. I piled a load of old chests on top of the hatch and tried to find a way out of the loft. Well, first I got myself pretty well lost. One loft seemed to lead to another, and some of them were pitch black, but at last I worked out a way round the edge of the house, so I'd always got a bit of light. Then I came across a little gable place with a wooden door. It had a padlock on it, but it wasn't much of a thing so I kicked it open.'

'And where were you?' I asked.

'I was on a flat roof with a parapet in front of me. There was a pitched roof with slates behind me and on each side, but I was standing on a flat space. I guessed I must be fac-ing the back of the house, so I went to the parapet to try and get down, but there wasn't a chance. From where I was I could see down on to a big garden and lawns. It was almost dark but I could see people all over the place. Some of them seemed to be dressed like actors.'

43

'How do you mean?' interrupted Holmes.

'They had strange kinds of clothes, all colours, and robes and things. They'd have seen me, even if I could have climbed down, but it was worse than that. Some of them were lighting a big fire in the middle of the garden. I reckoned I was best away from there, so I backed off and climbed over the slates to the front. It wasn't much better there.'

'Why not?' said Holmes.

'Well, when I looked over the front parapet I could see a long line of carriages in the drive. I supposed they'd brought the people who were drumming and chanting and I guessed some of them would have drivers waiting in them. But at least there wasn't a fire out front, so I'd have the darkness on my side. So I went over the parapet.'

'On your own! Without a rope or any assistance?' I exclaimed.

'Well, I didn't have a rope, doctor, so I had to do what I could. I could see the creeper was pretty heavy at the side of the porch, so I hung over the parapet and pulled at it. It seemed well rooted, but I wasn't sure it would carry me, so I went over backwards and pushed my feet in behind the stuff. Then when I let go the parapet I started to drop, but the creeper slowed me and, after a few feet, it held and I could begin climbing down.'

'That was pretty cool-headed of you,' said the Colonel, and shook his head wonderingly.

Jay told how he had clung to the creeper and clambered, inch by dangerous inch, down the darkened house-front, until he could drop the last few feet to the ground. In the shadow of the house he had crawled into the copse beside the drive.

'That was the really bad part,' he continued, as though his climb down the façade had been easy. 'I couldn't see an inch in the woods and I kept stumbling over, but in the end I got out on to the road.'

He paused. 'When I got on the road I ran as far as I could, but I didn't dare stay on the road in case they came after me with carriages, so I went over a hedge and hid down behind it and went to sleep. I thought they wouldn't be able to search properly in the dark and I couldn't find my way until daylight.'

'I'm astonished that you could sleep in the circumstances,' I remarked.

'Well, I couldn't at first. I was really hungry and I just couldn't sleep,' he said, and eyed the table. 'It was day when I woke. I heard shouting and I thought they'd come after me, but then I saw a boy with some cows down the bottom of the pasture. I reckoned he would show me the way to Winchester and I hoped he might have some food,' and he eyed the table again.

This time the Colonel took the point and rang for sandwiches. Further refreshed, Jay went on.

'I told the cowboy all that had happened to me. He spoke funny and I couldn't follow him at first, but in the end I managed to catch on to his accent. He said the house was haunted and nobody round about would go near it. He had some bread and cheese and he shared it with me.'

The experience of prolonged hunger seemed to have had the most lasting effect on the young millionaire, for he took another sandwich, having barely finished the first.

'I asked Charlie – that was his name – the way to Winchester and he said if I followed the road I was on I'd get here, but I was afraid to go on the road. I guessed I'd kind of stick out on an English country road. Then I thought of changing clothes with Charlie.'

'You didn't take the poor boy's clothes?' demanded his father.

'No, sir. I traded 'em. I gave Charlie my suit and half the money I had on me and all of my pear drops, but he gave the pear drops back and said I'd need them because it was a long walk and the sun was going to be hot. "Tez gonna be a rare hot un for May" ', he said, imitating his English friend.

'And so it was,' he continued. 'I walked the way Charlie showed me, across the fields until I came to the hills outside the town, but I had to stop and rest often. When I got here, I guessed they might be keeping watch so I came in and pretended I was Charlie with a message for my Pa, and that was worse than getting out of that house.'

His narrative concluded, Jay applied himself once more to the sandwiches, while the Colonel and I sat wondering at his matter-of-fact recital of his adventures. Holmes had his head back and his eyes closed, no doubt mulling over the details in Jay's story.

'The first opportunity I have I must reward young Charlie,' said Harden. 'He shall not lose by helping my son.'

I was pleased to hear the Colonel say so, for I had been proud that an English farm lad, living on pennies, had shown hospitality and friendship to the American millionaire's son, shared his meagre food and even returned the precious pear drops.

Holmes sat forward. 'Tell me,' he said, 'can you recognise the house again?'

'Why surely,' said Jay, from behind another sandwich.

'And could you take us there?' asked Holmes.

'I know the direction,' said the boy, 'but I don't know the road except the bit nearest the house.'

'But if we take you in the right direction, you can find the house?' persisted Holmes.

'Pretty certainly, yes, sir,' replied young Harden.

'Then we shall go there early tomorrow and see what more may be revealed,' said Holmes. 'Colonel, I suggest you arrange with the county police to send a couple of detective officers with us in the morning. Watson, do you think you could lay your hands on the Ordnance maps of this area? Jay, your adventures are over and I suspect you will be better off in bed.'

'But what about this Drew character?' demanded Colonel Harden.

'Drew's native heath is London,' said Holmes. 'He will have headed there as soon as he knew your son was gone. First let us see what that house may tell us in the morning.'

46

THE SIGN OF THE SERPENT

When we set out on our search next morning, Inspector Stubbington and Sergeant Morgan of the county police rode with Holmes, Harden and me in the carriage, while young Harden sat up with our driver, the better to direct him when he recognised his whereabouts.

From his inspection of maps the night before Holmes had drawn conclusions as to the location of the house. Now he questioned the two officers, describing the house and his belief that it had lain empty for well over a year.

They looked at each other, then Stubbington offered a suggestion.

'It sounds like Wayles Court,' he said. 'That's been empty a goodish time, too.'

'And where is Wayles Court?' asked Holmes.

'It's at the back of Greyhanger, sir,' said Morgan. 'Used to belong to old Mr Garton, the banker. That's been empty nearly four years now, it must be.'

'And do either of you know the house?' asked Holmes. 'Does it measure up to the boy's description?'

'I was there once, years ago,' said Stubbington, reflectively. 'It was a big garden party affair and there was Royalty about. It seems to me it did have pillars at the front and some kind of creeper growing up it. It could well be the place.'

'And it is four years since Mr Garton's death?' asked Holmes.

'Oh no, sir,' said Morgan. 'Old Mr Garton died nearly ten years gone. Then his son had it, but he spent all his father's money and got into bad trouble. He owed everyone and we was getting enquiries from Scotland Yard about him and that was when he shot himself. That was about four years ago.'

'Of course!' exclaimed Holmes, and smote his clenched fist on his thigh. 'It is Wayles Court without a doubt. Driver!' he called. 'Do you know the road to Greyhanger?'

'Yes sir,' replied the driver.

'Then you may take us directly there with all speed,' said Holmes, and leaning back in his seat he closed his eyes.

Colonel Harden and I shared our astonished expressions with the police officers, but I knew that to question Holmes would be fruitless, so we travelled in silence for some three miles.

Young Jay broke the silence with a cry of, 'This is the road! This is where I came out of the copse!'

Holmes was instantly alert, sitting forward with his eyes scanning the countryside on both sides of the road. In a moment the trees alongside us were interrupted by a pillared gateway.

'Do not turn in!' Holmes commanded our driver. 'We will walk up the drive.'

Hastily we disembarked and gathered in the gateway. Beyond the trees around the entrance, whose untrimmed branches hung into the roadway, a long drive curved away to the pillared portico, heavily festooned with the Virginia creeper that Jay had described. The gravel of the drive was old and dirty and had been heavily infested with clumps of weeds, but these had been largely crushed or torn out by carriage wheels whose marks were still fresh.

'That's it!' said Jay triumphantly, pointing at the house, and indeed we could even see the ragged track down the creeper where the boy had made his escape.

We walked up to the house and climbed the front steps. The paintwork of the handsome front door was well weathered and the brass fittings dulled. One half of the door was unfastened and slightly open. Holmes thrust it wide with his stick and we entered the hall.

It was a wide, graceful hall, floored in dark marble. From either side staircases curved up to a landing. Two sets of doors at the rear led into the house's interior and wide passages led off at each side.

The room was completely bare of furniture, but a huge diagram had been drawn in thick white chalk in the centre of the floor. It seemed to me to be the fortune-tellers' circle of the Zodiac. Here and there the lines of its pattern were spattered with thick candle grease. A tantalisingly familiar smell, sweet and pungent, hung in the air.

Sherlock Holmes stood beside the chalked outline while he gazed slowly around the hall. At length he turned back to the police officers.

'Inspector,' he said, 'may I suggest that you and your Sergeant search the upper floors, while Colonel Harden and the doctor and I search downstairs. Jay, go with the officers and assist them.'

'Right away, sir,' said Inspector Stubbington, 'but might I ask if you were expecting to find anything in particular?'

'It is a useful rule for the searcher,' said Holmes, 'to expect to find nothing. He will not then be disappointed if that is what he finds, nor will he be prejudiced in his views of anything that he does find.'

'No doubt you are right, sir,' said the Inspector, and he led his party upstairs.

Harden, Holmes and I began our inspection of the ground floor. The two doors at the rear of the hall both led into a wide sunlit drawing-room, with french windows opening onto a terrace. Here were more stains of candle grease and the same sweet smell. Now I realised it was the odour of incense that I had smelt in Indian temples years before.

The remainder of our tour yielded nothing until we reached the kitchen. Along one side a table bore row upon row of empty bottles, whose labels showed that they had held the best of wines and spirits. From beneath the table Holmes recovered a teaspoon and a label which bore the name of one of London's finest caterers and the pencilled name of a young lord well known in society.

'It seems that they have made a practice of meeting here,' said Holmes.

'Why do you say so?' I asked.

'The bottles,' said Holmes. 'The most recent are still clean, but the majority are coated with dust. It might be a pretty experiment to weigh the dust on each and thereby determine how many meetings have been held at this house, but it is not necessary. The date on this label shows us that they certainly met here in February.'

' "They"?' queried the Colonel.

'Mr Drew and what may be called his guests,' said Holmes. 'Come, gentlemen, I believe we have seen all that we need.'

We returned to the hall in time to meet the upstairs party. Inspector Stubbington drew Holmes aside and reported. 'There are ample signs of what I would call amorous activities in the bedrooms,' he said, 'and in one of them I found this.'

He took a folded paper from his pocket and passed it to my friend, who unfolded it carefully to reveal a pinch of silvery powder. Carrying it to a shaft of sunlight he examined it under his pocket-lens.

'This is excellent,' he said. 'Do you recall in which room you found it?'

'Yes, sir. The third bedroom in the west wing.'

'Pray take me there,' said Holmes, and he and the officer mounted the stairs.

They returned only a few minutes later, Holmes smiling to himself. 'Now,' he said, 'let us inspect the garden.'

We filed through the drawing-room on to the terrace, where Holmes paced up and down, sometimes stooping to touch a mark on the flagstones. At length he led us down a short flight of stone steps to the lawn.

Four years of neglect and a warm spring had left the lawn more like an unkempt meadow and it was easy to see that numbers of people had trampled it. A well-beaten path led from the steps to a circle of fresh ashes at the lawn's centre. As we followed it Holmes twice stooped to pick up and pocket small white objects.

The path of crushed grass circled the ashes and so did we, while Holmes kept his eyes fixed on them. 'Look, Watson,' he said, at one point, 'what do you make of that?'

In the edge of the ashes was a clear outline of a naked foot. 'A footprint!' I exclaimed. 'The naked foot of a woman or a youth.'

'Well done, Watson!' said Holmes. 'Evidently our revellers grew careless as the night wore on.'

We had almost completed the circuit when Holmes stopped again. 'May I trouble you, Sergeant, for a page from your pocket-book?' he asked Sergeant Morgan, and taking the proffered sheet he bent and scooped up another pinch of the silvery powder from the grass.

At last we had rounded the ashes and Holmes now leant across them, stirring their centre with his stick. From the deepest area of ash he extracted a blackened, twisted mass of wires and held them aloft from his stick.

'What do any of you suppose this was?' he enquired.

'Why, a birdcage!' said Jay.

'Exactly,' said Holmes, 'and unless I am much mistaken these are the remains of its occupants.' He shook the twisted wreckage and a lump of cinder fell to the ground and broke, revealing thin fragments of bone.

'The damned skunks!' exclaimed the boy, and his father turned away with a stronger oath.

'I can assure you,' said Holmes, 'that beside Mr Drew the skunk is a paragon of sweetness.'

He strode away towards the house and we followed. As we passed through the hall I ventured a question.

'So Drew has held some sort of Satanic ceremony here?' I asked.

'No, Watson,' he replied, and stopped by the chalked diagram. 'It had nothing to do with Satan. Look at that!' he commanded, and he struck his stick on to the chalked diagram on the floor. 'What do you understand that to be?'

'Why,' I said, 'it is a horoscope circle – the circle of the Zodiac, the sort of thing that fortune-tellers use. Surely it is merely a piece of stage dressing for their mumbo-jumbo?'

'Oh, Watson,' said Holmes, 'you see but you do not observe. The fortune-tellers' Zodiac has twelve divisions. This has thirteen.' He rapped his stick on the floor again. 'That,' he said, 'is the thirteenth sign – Ophiocus the Serpent Bearer.'

The two Hardens and I looked at him in astonishment.

'But what does it mean, sir?' asked young Jay.

'It means,' said Holmes, 'that what we are dealing with is not Satanism, but something much, much older.'

All of us were silent, gazing at the chalked figure. Holmes strode to the door and pushed it open.

'Winchester, I think, gentlemen. A late luncheon and perhaps a little illumination.'

A LITTLE ILLUMINATION

We rode quickly back to Winchester through the sunny noonday. Holmes was in great good humour, expatiating on wayside flowers and plants and explaining the geology of the region to young Harden, and I was pleased to see his mood. Seized of a new case, the spring of my friend's awesome intelligence would wind tighter and tighter and he would become increasingly taciturn as he sought to find a meaningful order in the facts presented to him. Once he had achieved an understanding of them, the great spring unwound and he became as delightful and witty a companion as one might wish.

After luncheon, when Mrs Harden and her daughters had withdrawn, we gathered around a decanter of brandy. Holmes went carefully through his pockets and laid on the table before him, item by item, the objects he had acquired at Wayles Court – the two paper packets of the silvery powder, a teaspoon, the caterer's label and two small white feathers. He arranged them in a row, then looked up at Colonel Harden.

'Colonel Harden,' he said, 'you have been very patient in awaiting my explanation of the bizarre events that have surrounded your family, but whereas before I had only suspicions, the evidence at Wayles Court has enabled me to draw some firm conclusions.' He gestured towards his little row of exhibits. 'Perhaps,' he said, 'you will permit me to explain my reasoning.'

'Fire away, Mr Holmes,' said the Colonel. 'The floor is yours,' and he passed him a cigar-case.

'Thank you,' said Holmes, selecting a cigar. 'I think, perhaps, I should begin with Drew. Your son's extraordinary ear for voices enabled me to be quite sure that the architect of your persecution was Drew.'

He paused while he lit his cigar and drew it to a steady glow. 'It is a little short of four years since I tried conclusions with the late Professor Moriarty in Switzerland. Watson has published the story in his little melodrama "The Final Problem". That it was final for the Professor was my good fortune. My misfortune was that one of Moriarty's gang, perhaps the most dangerous of them, was aware that I had survived the encounter. As a result I was unable to return to England until I saw the opportunity to ensnare Moriarty's henchman and ensure my own safety.

'Before my confrontation with the Professor I had supplied Scotland Yard with a very complete dossier on Moriarty's criminal empire and I had every hope that, by the time of my return, the majority of his lieutenants would be languishing in prison. That was not, alas, entirely so. Drew and his little band escaped the law, largely because of the unwillingness of witnesses to testify against them.'

'I do not recall that you have ever mentioned Drew before,' I remarked.

'Very probably not,' said Holmes, 'but I have known of him for a good many years. He was, for some time, a Sergeant in the Detective Division at Scotland Yard, and was well thought of by his superiors as an industrious and intelligent officer. He spoke several languages and had a quick brain. At the same time, his immediate colleagues were becoming aware that Drew's character was deeply flawed. He is one of those dark creatures whose only real pleasure in life is derived from inflicting pain on others.

'Drew came close to disaster when a street-boy died under his interrogation in the cells at Cannon Row, but he was able to cover that up. His career ended when he was found to be involved with a gang of race-course crooks.'

54

'The Benson case!' exclaimed Inspector Stubbington.

'The same,' said Holmes. 'Drew and a number of his colleagues were imprisoned, but he emerged to a new career with Moriarty's gang. The Professor's own descent into crime had been brought about by too great an affection for wealth, and Drew showed Moriarty a way of ensuring a constant flow of money into his pockets, a flow that the law would find it very difficult to interrupt. Drew's efforts financed the huge expansion of Moriarty's influence that made him such a threat to the whole country.'

'But you disposed of Moriarty,' I said.

'Very true, Watson, but I did not dispose of Drew, and with his master gone he was free to continue his schemes for his own profit.'

Holmes picked up the caterer's label. 'When I heard the name "Garton" this morning I recalled a victim of that name in my dossier for the Yard. It confirmed my identification of Drew and indicated Wayles Court as our destination. It is evident from this, and from the ranks of dusty bottles, that since young Garton's death Drew's gang has been making use of Wayles Court for regular gatherings.'

'But what went on there, Mr Holmes?' asked the Inspector. 'You said something older than Satan.'

'Satanism,' said Holmes, 'is a product of Christianity, a perverse heresy that centres its worship around the Christian Devil and its philosophy around the negation of every Christian ideal. Before the coming of Christ there were other systems of belief, one of which was paramount in the ancient world. You have heard of the Eleusinian Mysteries?'

'But that was a philosophy of spiritual enlightenment!' I expostulated. 'Surely, many early Christians felt able to remain under the vow of Eleusis?'

'True,' Holmes replied. 'The heralds required only those with clean hands and a clean heart to approach the initiation. Nero travelled to Eleusis, intent on initiation, but when he heard the heralds he reconsidered his position and did not put himself forward. It is said that the initiation would drive unsuitable candidates to madness.'

'What was the initiation, Mr Holmes?' asked Jay Harden.

'The vow of secrecy was absolute,' Holmes replied. 'The ritual has not come down to us in any authentic form, but we know a little about it. For example, we know that some variants of the cult employed a Zodiac of thirteen houses, based on the cycles of the moon, rather than the more common solar Zodiac of twelve houses.'

'But what have Zodiacs and the worship of Demeter at Eleusis got to do with Drew's racket?' demanded the Colonel.

'The worship of Demeter – the Mother Goddess, the goddess of fertility and the earth's bounty – was central to the Eleusinian cult,' said Holmes, 'and she is found in all the pantheons of the ancient world. She is Anu, she is Isis, she is Diana. She was the Magna Mater, upon whose temple in London the Christians built the church of Magnus the Martyr. But she was not only the goddess of life and fertility. She was also the goddess of death. She is Hecate, she is Ceridwen of the Celts, she is the Gaels' Cailleach – the Hag with Seven Husbands. In Ireland she is the Morrigan – the goddess of warriors' doom who rides the winds of the battlefield with her blood-spattered raven wings.'

He paused. 'With the spread of Christianity the cult of the Great Mother was driven underground. Flourishing only in the dark, the dark side of the belief became ascendant. It became a cult of death and power, of curses and evil, and its once joyous celebration of fertility became an obsession with perverse forms of eroticism.'

Holmes picked up a scrap of white feather from the table. 'The dove,' he said, 'was one of the sacred symbols of light and peace and love at Eleusis, but at Wayles Court they burned live doves in a cage. 30th April was May Eve, the old fertility festival of Beltane, and so Drew assembled his prospects and lured them into shameful rituals that unleashed their darker desires.'

'I don't see how he would make much out of organising drunken orgies for the rich,' commented the Colonel.

'You should understand that Drew possesses a wide knowledge of peculiar philosophies and obscure religions, most particularly those whose rituals are dramatic, violent and erotic. London is full of wealthy young men and women who are bored by society. They read Huysmans and they look for the kind of excitements he describes. Sooner or later they find their way to Drew. Under the pretence of being a scholar – or even a believer – he lures his marks into behaviour which makes them his prey.'

'But how?' asked Harden.

'The secret of Drew's vile business is contained in these,' said Holmes and he picked up the two folded papers.

'Drugs?' I hazarded.

'No,' said Holmes, 'though certain drugs are a part of his paraphernalia. These are a chemical of much simpler action.'

Unwrapping the sachets he tapped their contents into an ashtray and stabbed his cigar into the heap of glittering powder. A blaze of white flame burst in the ashtray, illuminating the whole room with a brilliant light, and causing all of us to recoil.

'Flash powder!' exclaimed Colonel Harden. 'He had a photographer in attendance!'

'Exactly, Colonel. Spillages of magnesium powder as used by photographers in their flash-pans. I had little doubt of its meaning when Inspector Stubbington first produced it to me, and a brief examination of a bedroom floor revealed the marks of a photographer's tripod in the dust.'

'Blackmail by photographs!' exclaimed the inspector. 'The filthy scoundrel!'

'And Drew's victims,' said Holmes, 'would never complain. They faced bankruptcy and even death rather than reveal what Drew's pictures of them showed.'

'But what has this blackmailing swine got to do with me and my family? Jay and my daughters are too young and have no hand on my money. It doesn't figure,' said the Colonel.

Sherlock Holmes rose and opened a casement to let the smoke of his demonstration dissipate. He turned and leant against the sill, his tall figure dark against the sunlit window.

'If you and yours had been intended victims,' he said, 'you would have received cunningly disguised invitations to one of Drew's gatherings, but you did not. You have received only threats, escalating to the abduction of your son. Drew does not regard you as a potential asset, Colonel Harden. For some reason he regards you as a very real threat.'

The Colonel chewed his cigar for some minutes while a range of expressions passed across his face. 'Look here,' he said at last, 'we've been all around this, Mr Holmes. There is no way that I represent a threat to anyone in England, let alone this blackmailing skunk Drew. Now, you have worked out a great deal. You were right about Jay and you're obviously right about what happened at that house. Can you tell me –'

'No,' interrupted Holmes. 'If you are about to ask why you are a threat to Drew or why, at least, he believes you to be, I cannot tell you, nor do I believe I shall ever be able to tell you.'

'Now see here,' said Harden, 'I have nothing but admiration for you, Mr Holmes, since I've seen you at work, but I don't take kindly to refusals. If it's a question of fees –'

Holmes stopped him with a raised hand. 'My fees', he said, 'never vary, save when I remit them entirely, and they are not the problem. There is an insuperable objection to my investigating Drew's harassment of you, Colonel. My enquiries must end here.'

The rest of us had been dumbstruck by Holmes' first denial; now even the Colonel was silent. Holmes returned to his seat by the table.

'Let me put it another way,' he said. 'You brought me here, Colonel, to deal with the abduction of your boy. You have allowed that I was correct in my deductions. Through his own pluck and enterprise Jay is free and unharmed. We know who did it and, if you require vengeance, you can have it. I can run Drew to earth for you and charge him under the Offences Against the Person Act. Jay's evidence will convict him and he will return to prison for a long time, but I do not advise that course.'

'Why the blazes not?' growled Harden.

'Because it will not reveal the answer to your question, nor will it stop the harassment of your family by Drew's cronies, whether now or on any other visit to these shores.'

'Then what am I to do?' demanded the Colonel.

'For the safety of yourself and your family I can give you only one answer – leave England at the first opportunity.'

Harden stood up and paced right around the table, clearing his throat several times as he did so. At last he came back to his seat, but remained standing.

'Mr Holmes,' he said, 'my Pa, J. Wayne Harden, came from nowhere and built a great plantation and a great fortune. Never in all his life did he flinch from any man, lie to any man nor twist any man. He taught me always that a man must do not what he wants to do, nor even less what others expect him to do, but only what he knows he must do.'

He cleared his throat again. 'We freed our slaves before the war because my Pa believed that slavery stained the face of a Christian nation, but when the shooting began at Fort Sumter and I asked his advice he said, "Slavery is wrong, son, but the right of your State to be wrong is being threatened." That's all he said, but it was enough for me. Like Robert E. Lee I followed my native State with my sword and my life.'

He paused and we were all silent in the face of his strong emotion.

'I have never flinched from Secessionists, Abolitionists, the army of the Union nor the damned Ku-Klux-Klan,' he declaimed, 'and no filthy hog of a blackmailer is going to drive me out of England. This varmint has threatened my children and stolen my boy. I don't give a damn what it

59

takes, Mr Holmes, but I am staying here and taking my pictures. Your police can protect my family and when Drew's scum come after me, you can trap him. Does that suit you?'

Holmes's eyes had begun to glow during the Colonel's speech and now he sprang to his feet and shook the old soldier warmly by the hand.

'Magnificent, Colonel!' he cried. 'No one has any right to ask it of you, but if that is your wish, that is what we shall do.'

Colonel Harden took his seat and replenished his brandy. The decanter went round the table, then Inspector Stubbington spoke.

'How will you find this Drew, Mr Holmes?' he asked.

'With this,' said Holmes, and brandished the teaspoon that lay in front of him.

9

PRIESTESS AND PRIEST

A plan of campaign was made that night. It was agreed that the county police would guard the Harden family closely and escort Mrs Harden and her children to London. Once there, Scotland Yard would take over responsibility for their safety. Meanwhile the Colonel would pursue his photographic itinerary, but under a guard provided by Holmes.

Next morning all of the arrangements were confirmed by telegram and, by mid-afternoon, Holmes and I were ready to return to London. Our bags had been loaded into a cab when Holmes looked at his watch.

'It is a little early for tea,' he remarked, 'but I fancy taking it in Winchester. Cabby, be so good as to deliver our bags to the station, for the London train. Watson, would you to care to join me in a stroll before tea?'

Completely bemused by Holmes' change of our programme, I joined him in taking our farewells of the Hardens. 'Do not,' Holmes told the Colonel, 'step outside this hotel, nor let your family do so, until all arrangements for your safety are in place.'

For an hour or so Holmes and I perambulated the highways and byways of Winchester. Those who did not know him would have sworn that my friend had nothing on his mind but the passing of a sunny afternoon in a curious and interesting city, but I was agog to know what element of the Harden case he was pursuing. He vouchsafed me no indication, and I knew it to be useless to question him.

Towards four o'clock we found ourselves in one of the small streets that surround the city's cathedral. Holmes paused outside a confectioner's and drew my attention to the display of cakes in the window.

'We might,' he said, 'refresh ourselves here both pleasurably and profitably,' and he turned into the door.

The place was larger than its modest frontage suggested. While the door gave immediate access to the confectionary shop, there was a tea-room behind. Several of its tables were already occupied by youths whom I took to be pupils of the city's college.

Holmes and I found a corner table and ordered tea. Our order was, I may say, filled to the full, and for a while we plied our attention to a table loaded with teacakes, bread and butter, tarts and a magnificent fruit cake.

'This is very agreeable,' I said at last, 'but is there some reason other than refreshment for us being here?'

'The first reason,' said Holmes, helping himself to another slice of fruit cake, 'is that we were being observed at the hotel. A person across the street was having the most extreme difficulties in retying his shoelace. I thought it better to lead him astray and lose him in the side streets, which I have done. The second has to do with this,' and he drew from his pocket the teaspoon from Wayles Court.

'You will observe', he remarked, 'that the handle bears the initials K.C.C. A few moments with a commercial directory this morning revealed that there is a Kensall's Catering Company in Winchester, and the spoon in your saucer confirms that we have come to the right address inasmuch as it bears the same monogram. It is not, I think, unreasonable to hope that the proprietor of this excellent teashop has supplied refreshments for one or more of the revellers at Wayles Court.'

As the waitress began clearing our table, Holmes asked, 'Would it be possible for me to have a word with the proprietor?'

'The owner?' said the young woman. 'Mrs Kensall? We're very busy at tea-time, but I'll see if she's available.'

The tea-room had, indeed, quite filled up since our arrival, but soon we saw an ample lady in a long white apron making her way through the tables towards us, much after the manner of a ship in full sail. She halted by our table, arms akimbo, and fixed Holmes with a hostile glare.

'I understand,' she said, as we both rose, 'that you gentlemen have a complaint.'

'Certainly not!' exclaimed Holmes. 'There has evidently been a misunderstanding. My friend and I have been excellently served. Could you spare a moment to answer a few simple questions, madam?'

She seemed a little mollified. 'If you're travellers,' she announced, 'you've picked the worst time and I don't see representatives except by appointment.'

'All that I represent is the cause of justice,' said my friend. 'I am Sherlock Holmes and this is Dr Watson. I have here a teaspoon which I believe may belong to you.'

Mrs Kensall narrowed her eyes shrewdly. 'You didn't come from London to return one of my lost teaspoons, Mr Sherlock Holmes. You've come about that affair at Wayles Court. You'd better come with me.'

We followed her to a private door which led into her office. When we were seated she said, 'Now, what's your interest in Wayles Court, Mr Holmes?'

'I had not said that I had any interest in Wayles Court, but you are, of course, correct. How did you divine the nature of my enquiries?'

Mrs Kensall folded her hands on the desk. 'Three days ago I catered for a party at Wayles Court,' she said. 'My lads and girls who worked there threatened to leave afterwards through the things they saw and the insults they had to put up with. Now you turn up in my teashop, as large as life, investigating something. We don't see much excitement down here in Hampshire, Mr Holmes, not within three days.'

Holmes smiled broadly. 'How very astute of you,' he said. 'My interest lies in tracking down the person or persons who held that infamous party. When I found your teaspoon I hoped that you had supplied some of the refreshments. I am delighted to hear that you catered for the entire event. May I ask who engaged your services?'

Mrs Kensall's eyes hardened. 'A snivelling little whelp called Culbone. He came to me six weeks ago and gave his orders. He said it was a spring party for a religious society that he represented, the lying little toad.'

'Culbone,' said Holmes, musingly. 'Was he a slight, red-faced man with a rather prominent nose and a nervous manner?'

'The very same,' said our hostess. 'He said that he was secretary of the society.'

'Do you have an address for the society?' asked Holmes.

'Certainly I do,' she replied. 'We don't do business on the side here. He paid in cash, but I had an address and I wrote to him to confirm his orders, so it must be real.'

She turned about and selected a large ledger from a row behind her; placing it on the desk, she began to leaf through it.

'Here we are,' she said at last, and turned the volume so that we could see the page. 'Mr Alfred Culbone, function at Wayles Court, Greyhanger, 30th April, and the address is there – the Society of Saint Ophiocus, 14 Norreys Lane, The Strand, London.'

'Excellent!' exclaimed Holmes and copied the address into his pocket-book. 'Tell me, Mrs Kensall, if the question is not indelicate, what so upset your employees at Wayles Court?'

'According to this Culbone's orders, I supplied four girls to prepare and lay out the food and four waiters and four waitresses to serve his guests. Now they were all experi-enced, they've seen the aristocracy at play and they're used to things getting a little bit out of hand and they know how to comport themselves, but it wasn't like that at Wayles Court. It was much worse.'

'In what way?' asked Holmes.

'To put it bluntly, Mr Holmes, they're used to having to ignore certain propositions, but at Wayles Court they

64

were more than propositioned – they were mauled by drunken hooligans who had come there for indecent purposes.'

'I see,' said Holmes. 'Did any of them complain to the police?'

'I persuaded them not to,' said Mrs Kensall, 'in the interests of my business, but I didn't feel right about it.'

'That is probably just as well,' said Holmes. 'Who knows how it might reflect on your business if it were to become generally known.' He rose from his chair. 'You have been a great help to me,' he said. 'I thank you and I shall remember, if I return to Winchester, where to find the city's finest fruit cake.'

As we made for the railway station I asked, 'How do you come to know this Culbone?'

'Because,' he replied, 'Culbone is a village in the West of England, closely adjacent to the Somerset village of Porlock.'

It was evidently all the answer I was going to receive, though it was completely meaningless to me.

Early next day we took a cab from Baker Street intent, as Holmes expressed it, on 'visiting old friends'. Our first call was at a large public house in the northern part of the City. We left the cab waiting and I followed Holmes down the side of the public house, where a horse ramp led down to the towpath of a canal. A few yards along the canal stood a weatherbeaten warehouse building, with a flight of rickety wooden steps up to its upper storey.

At the top of the steps a door led us into a long, low hall, formed from the entire top storey of the building. As we entered we were immediately aware of the heavy reek of perspiration, mixed with the odours of liniment and leather. Young men in athletic clothing were hard at work, exercising on a number of devices.

At the far end of the room a full-sized boxing ring was rigged and there two lads were slugging it out valiantly. A small group stood beside the ring, occasionally offering encouragement or criticism. One of these, in a corduroy jacket and billycock hat, turned towards us as we approached the ring.

'Well!' he exclaimed loudly. 'What a sight for sore eyes! Mr Sherlock Holmes himself and Dr Watson at his side. Good day to you, gentlemen!'

The man's easy familiarity with our names made me look again. He was broad-chested and evidently a former prize-fighter. Two very sharp, bright eyes watched me from above a pugilist's battered nose.

'McMurdo's the name you're seeking, doctor,' he said to me. 'We met when I was doing a spot of minding at Pondicherry Lodge a few years back. Mind you, I've known Mr Holmes a bit longer than that. Ever since he nearly grassed me at Alison's rooms on me own benefit night. They told me you was dead, Mr Holmes,' he said, turning back to my friend.

'They exaggerated,' said Holmes, smiling. 'It is a pleasure to see you again, McMurdo. I was told you had adopted the disreputable career of a trainer.'

'I told 'em,' said the boxer. 'I said, "I shall believe as Sherlock Holmes is dead when Sherlock Holmes himself tells me so." Now, what brings you my way, gentlemen?'

'A "spot of minding", as you so neatly put it,' said Holmes.

'Then we'd best retire to my office,' said McMurdo, and showed us into a little cubicle in one corner of his gymnasium.

For a few minutes McMurdo explained his retirement from active fighting. 'When I fought Thompson, the New Zealander, for a red kettle and a purse there was three times when he nearly had me. Came almost as near as you did, Mr Holmes, so I thought it time to hang up the gloves, and I can't say I'm sorry. Now then, what about your bit of business?'

Succinctly, Holmes explained Colonel Harden's situation. McMurdo listened silently. When Holmes had finished the trainer opened the door of his cubicle and bellowed three names down the hall.

'You'll want three,' he said, returning to his seat, 'and these three are as good as I can give you.'

A moment later three young men appeared at the door. McMurdo introduced them. 'They're hard,' he said, 'and quick, and they knows how to take discipline. Your man couldn't be in better hands.'

Holmes explained the task to the three and paid them sufficient coin for their immediate needs. 'Make sure', he told them, 'that any attack, or any attempted attack, on Colonel Harden is reported to me by telegraph. I wish also to be informed of the Colonel's movements every single day, and when he moves his lodgings I wish to know in advance.'

The trio went about their business and we took our farewell of McMurdo. At the next post office Holmes wired to Harden to expect McMurdo's men and we moved on to our second call of the day.

10

MR CULBONE'S SOCIETY

I was not surprised to find that the Society of Saint Ophiocus had its headquarters near to Holywell Street, where the pedlars of obscenities have been entrenched for many years. No doubt the proximity made it easier for Drew's victims to find their nemesis.

The premises of the society had been a double-fronted shop, but the windows were now backed by green blinds and bore only the figure of the Serpent Bearer in gilt. A fresh brass plate announced the address to be the society's offices and gave the secretary's name as Culbone.

A shop bell rang as we entered. Immediately inside the door was a waiting area, set with chairs and two tables. Bookshelves lined the side walls. A step down led to a rail, behind which screens concealed the office area of the premises.

At the sound of the bell a voice called from behind the screens. 'Do please take a seat. I shall be with you in one moment.'

Holmes smiled to himself and turned to examine the bookshelves. Most of the volumes were obscure texts on arcane subjects. Necromancy and astrology were covered in great detail. There were foreign works, in the original and in translation, many by authors of whom I had never heard.

Knowing my friend's interest in the Celtic languages, I drew his attention to one volume, *La Vraie Langue Celtique* by one Abbé Boudet. Holmes snorted.

'That reverend gentleman', he said, 'believes that the original language of the Celtic tribes was English! Like the British Israelites, whose nonsense is also here, he draws no distinction between Iberian and Celt, Saxon, Dane and Norman.'

'The British Israelites?' I said.

'A curious sect who believe that Britain is occupied by the descendants of the Twelfth Tribe of ancient Israel, and manage to ignore the considerable evidence of our polyglot heritage. If the devotees of Saint Ophiocus can believe this rubbish, it must be very easy for Drew to ensnare them.'

We turned at the sound of footsteps. A small, red-faced man, with spectacles bridging a prominent nose, had emerged from the office area.

'Can I assist you, gentlemen?' he asked, then blanched as Holmes faced him.

'Good morning, Freddy,' said Holmes. 'Watson, let me introduce my old and valued friend, Freddy Porlock, Mr Porlock, or Culbone as he now styles himself, was once my eyes and ears within Professor Moriarty's councils. You have wandered once more from the straight and narrow, Freddy.'

'Mr Holmes,' said Porlock, with a gulp, 'I was not expecting to see you. As to my employment here, since the Professor's unfortunate demise and your disappearance, I have been forced to do the best I can.'

'A poor best indeed,' remarked Holmes. 'As to Moriarty, the only unfortunate aspect of his end was its timing. It was some thirty years too late. Now, what of your new master? Tell me about Mr Drew.'

'I daren't, Mr Holmes. I really daren't!' Porlock glanced around him fearfully. 'If Drew was to come in and see you, it'd be all up with me. He knows you, Mr Holmes, and he's a terrible man when he's crossed.'

Holmes slipped his watch from his pocket and glanced at it. 'It wants a quarter of noon,' he said. 'Watson and I will retire to the public house at the corner of the street. I shall expect to see you there at noon, when you close this office for luncheon. There is money in this for you, Freddy, but if that no longer exerts its old attraction, I might have to refer to Scotland Yard certain documents of dubious penmanship.'

Porlock stood pale and silent. My friend turned on his heel. 'Come, Watson,' he said. 'Freddy, do not fail our luncheon appointment!'

It was a minute after noon when Porlock joined us in a corner of the public house. Despite the warm day, he wore an overcoat with upturned collar and gloves. His constant nervous glances sideways showed that he was still afraid of being seen in conversation with Holmes.

'Now,' said Holmes, when our guest had slid into a seat and a drink had been supplied, 'here are two things, Freddy. On the one hand you can, if you will, supply me with useful information; on the other hand, you can answer to Scotland Yard for your less than expert penmanship. Which is it to be?'

Porlock drank deeply and leaned across the table. 'You did say there would be money in it for me, Mr Holmes, didn't you?'

'If you require payment, you will be paid at the old rate,' said Holmes, 'but only if I can make use of your information.'

'What is it you want to know, Mr Holmes?'

'Your new master – Drew – his business is blackmail. Why, then, is he interested in Colonel Harden?'

'Blackmail, Mr Holmes? Surely not. I'm certain I'd know if there was anything like that in the wind.'

Holmes' hand shot out, pinning Porlock's left wrist to the table. With delicate care he pulled the glove from the little man's hand by its fingers.

'It is not unusual to carry gloves in summer,' he remarked, 'but the wearing of them suggests concealment. There', he announced, 'is the evidence that, three days ago, you were in Hampshire, taking disgusting photographs to support Drew's demands upon his victims –

stains of photographer's nitrate on your fingers. Must I unveil the recent burn on your left thumb and forefinger – the marks of a hot flash-pan? Do not waste my time, Freddy. For all I care you may just as readily stand in Winchester Guildhall as a blackmailer rather than the Bailey as a forger.'

Porlock withdrew his stained hand and slid it into his pocket. 'I hadn't no choice, Mr Holmes. That Drew's a monster when he's crossed. But I don't know what he wants with the American, that's the truth.'

'Drew has had my client followed and threatened for weeks. He has arranged for a shot to be fired at him. He himself played a part in the abduction of Colonel Harden's son. None of this can have to do with blackmail, but Drew has made endless efforts to frighten the Colonel. It is evidently of the first importance to Drew, and I cannot believe that you know nothing of it.'

Porlock gulped nervously at his beer, his eyes never leaving Holmes' face. At last he wiped his mouth and appeared to come to a decision. He leaned across the table and spoke very softly.

'It was something the Professor was looking for, years ago. Sometimes I heard him say that if he had it he could control the whole world.'

'And what was it?' said Holmes.

'I don't know, Mr Holmes, I don't know. The Professor used to call it the Devil's Grail and then he would laugh. He had a dreadful laugh,' he said, reminiscently.

'I am sure,' said my friend, 'that you know more than that,' and a coin appeared between his fingers as if by magic.

Porlock's eyes slid from Holmes' face to the coin and back again. 'The old rate?' he asked.

'The old rate – for the truth,' confirmed Holmes.

Porlock licked his lips. 'I first heard of it years ago. The Professor used to talk about it sometimes. He said it was the greatest treasure in England.'

'And what about Drew?' demanded Holmes. 'How did he come to seek it?'

71

'The Professor used to discuss it with him. Drew must know what it is, they talked about it often. Drew used to say, "I'm the best detective in London – I'll find it for you!" and the old Professor would laugh his nasty laugh and say, "It was hidden so only someone like me could find it, and there is no other like me!" '

He paused and Holmes said, 'What else have you heard?'

'Only that someone else had tried to find it and couldn't,' said Porlock.

'Who was that?' asked Holmes, sharply.

'The Professor once said that Henry Yates had tried and tried, but he never got his hands on it, only someone like the Professor could find it.'

'And who,' said Holmes, 'is Henry Yates?'

'I never heard of him before or since, Mr Holmes, I tell you honestly.'

'What has Drew said about it?' demanded my friend.

'Only as he's going to have it and the American shan't stop him. Drew says if he isn't stopped soon, he'll have to be stopped at Glastonbury.'

'At Glastonbury?' repeated Holmes, and his eyes opened very wide. 'He said Glastonbury?'

'Definitely,' said Porlock, and his eyes were roaming round nervously. 'Look, Mr Holmes, I daren't stay here any more and that's all I can tell you.'

'Very well,' said Holmes, and laid a coin on the table. He took out another and held it. 'The old rates, Freddy, for information on Drew's movements and anything he says that relates to Colonel Harden. A note to Baker Street will always find me. But mind you, Freddy, play me false and Scotland Yard shall have you.'

'You know me, Mr Holmes,' said Porlock, and grabbing the two coins he slid out of his seat and scuttled away.

We finished our drinks and left. In a cab on the way to Baker Street, Holmes looked at me quizzically.

'You are silent, Watson. Does Porlock's information raise no train of thought?'

72

'To be frank,' I replied, 'I was thinking that you bullied the little wretch somewhat.'

'My dear old friend,' exclaimed Holmes, 'I am sorry indeed that you should perceive me in such a light! Porlock has two great weaknesses – money and dishonesty. If he can, he will trade the second for the first. He is fully capable of betraying his connection with me to Drew for money and passing me untrue information for more money. I am afraid that the only guarantee against such a manœuvre is to ensure that he is too frightened to try it. Now he has committed himself we can, I think, rely on him in future.'

His explanation mollified me somewhat and I asked, 'Who is this Henry Yates?'

Holmes laughed. 'At present I have only a slender surmise, but I shall soon know better.'

He rapped with his stick on the cab's roof. 'Cabby!' he called. 'Go by the British Museum and pause there!'

At the museum he leaped down from the cab. 'Carry on to Baker Street,' he told me, 'and tell Mrs Hudson that I shall have my dinner at the usual time.'

He began to stride away, but I called after him. 'The usual time? What time is that?'

'Why, when she sees me, Watson – when she sees me!' and with a cheery wave of his stick he was gone.

11

RHYMES AND CLOCK-JACKS

Holmes was as good as his word; neither Mrs Hudson nor I saw him until late that evening, when he returned from the British Museum with a keen appetite. I knew this to be a sign that he believed himself to be making progress with his enquiries, for often he would not eat at all when his line of thought was unproductive.

Over our delayed dinner I questioned him. 'Has the British Museum revealed to you the identity of Henry Yates?' I asked, jocularly.

'Yes, indeed,' he replied. 'Not only do I know who he was, together with altogether unnecessary details of his many marriages, I have also confirmed that Jack Horner's thumb played a part in this story four and a half centuries ago.'

'Four hundred and fifty years ago!' I exclaimed, and then the light broke. 'Henry Yates was Henry the Eighth?'

'Congratulations, Watson. Porlock is not, it seems, a student of history and misunderstood Moriarty's joking reference.'

'But surely, Henry would have had the resources to find it if it could be found?'

'Henry's approach was, as ever, less than subtle. You will recall that, having fallen out with the Pope over the question of his remarriage, he used the opportunity to appoint himself head of the Church in England and demanded that English priests signify their agreement. Those who disagreed were at best deprived of office, at worst executed, and their abbeys, monasteries and manors went to bribe the King's allies and enrich the Royal treasury.'

'But what on earth has Jack Horner's thumb got to do with it?' I asked.

Holmes laughed and recited the rhyme: 'Little Jack Horner sat in a corner, eating his Christmas pie. He put in his thumb and pulled out a plum, saying, "Oh, what a good boy am I!" '

I stared and he laughed again. 'Horner,' he said, 'was a supporter of the King in Somerset. When Henry destroyed the abbey at Glastonbury, the deeds of its wealthy manors were sent to London in Horner's care. It was quite customary at the time to bake a pie-crust over important documents, so that they could not be tampered with in transit, but somehow Horner became the lord of a Manor shortly after. Popular opinion attributed his good fortune to a dextrous thumb, though it might have been a reward for serving on the jury that hanged the Abbot of Glastonbury'.

'The Abbot was hanged?' I said.

'Oh yes. I have seen Chancellor Cromwell's note – "Item: the Abbot of Glaston and his accomplices to be tried and hanged" – and Cromwell was a man of his word.'

'Might not the Abbot have surrendered the secret of this Devil's Grail before his execution?' I asked.

'Certainly,' said Holmes, 'and the more so since it might have saved his life, but the documents I have seen show that something that was sought at Glastonbury was not found and we have Moriarty's word for it that that was the case.'

'What will you do now?' I enquired.

'I must continue my historic researches, and you must receive any messages from Porlock or from McMurdo's lads and relay them to me. In the meantime, please take a knife and Hornerise Mrs Hudson's estimable blackcurrant pie.'

For several days our routine was the same. Holmes left early in the morning, usually for the British Museum or some other depository of ancient records, while I spent the days at home, awaiting messages, not daring to take more than a brief stroll in Regent's Park by way of recreation. Holmes returned later each evening, growing more taciturn as his researches failed to bear fruit and often sitting with his pipe into the small hours. Telegrams from Harden's bodyguard told us only that he was progressing westward from Winchester to Romsey, Salisbury, Amesbury, Avebury and Stanton Drew. There was no word from Porlock.

I had begun to believe that we were condemned to such dull days indefinitely when there came a message from McMurdo's men. Colonel Harden had gone to Wells, intending to visit Glastonbury next. I passed it on to Holmes at the British Museum and that night he showed me the reply he had sent:

REMAIN AT WELLS UNTIL I ARRIVE STOP GLASTONBURY IS THE DANGER POINT STOP HOLMES

'I had not intended to travel west until my researches were complete,' complained Holmes, 'but the Colonel's movements may force our hand.'

He had already left Baker Street the following morning when the post brought an anonymous note:

D has the American watched at Wells. He says he will follow him if he goes to Glastonbury.

It was evidently from Porlock, and I sent it at once to Holmes by messenger. To my surprise he arrived within the hour.

Striding into our sitting-room he rubbed his hands and smiled. 'I have wired Harden that we shall arrive in Wells tomorrow,' he said. 'Let us take advantage of our leisure and go out to luncheon.'

Over our meal he was in high good spirits, talking of everything but the Harden case, and it was evident to me that he had made progress with his enquiries though he gave me no more information.

We departed for Wells early the next morning and one of McMurdo's men met us at the railway station. 'Colonel Harden is at the cathedral with the boys,' he told us. 'He wants to see the clock strike.'

'To see the clock strike!' I exclaimed, but Holmes laughed. 'As usual,' he said, 'it takes an American to remind the British of the remarkable things that our island contains. If we hurry, Watson, we too may be able to see the clock strike.'

We found Colonel Harden in the north transept of the cathedral, accompanied by McMurdo's men and surrounded by a small group which seemed to consist of other foreigners and a few local children. He hailed us as we approached.

'Good-day, gentlemen. You are just in time,' he said, and pulling out his watch he checked it against the huge clock on the west wall. I looked up and gasped in astonishment.

Over us hung the most extraordinary clock I have ever seen. Its dial, more than six feet across, was a mass of decorations and numbers, indicating the phases of the moon and the state of the planets in their orbits. To show the time of day it had an outer circle of twenty-four divisions, around which moved a large star, while a smaller star moved round an inner circle of sixty parts.

As we looked, the smaller star completed its circuit. Above and to the left of the great dial a quaint little figure jerked its wooden leg forwards and backwards, striking it against a bell hung beneath, then repeated the movement with the other leg to ring another bell. Eight times the manikin struck his bells, while a whirring sound came from the clock itself.

Now four figures appeared in a cavity above the clock-face, two mounted, armed knights riding clockwise and two anti-clockwise. At each pass one or another of them was struck back on his horse by an opponent's sword.

I gaped, as wonderstruck as any of the children around us, as this miniature battle whirred to an end and the protagonists disappeared. Adults smiled and murmured with pleasure, while the children laughed with delight at the ingenious show.

'There are few clocks so old,' said Harden, pocketing his watch, 'and none so clever, unless it is the great clock at Strasbourg. It awes me, gentlemen, to think that clock was set going a century before America was discovered.'

'It was made,' said Holmes, 'by Peter Lightfoot, a monk of Glastonbury, more than five hundred years ago. They were curious and learned men, with many strange skills. I entirely understand your fascination with it, Colonel, but we must now talk of other aspects of Glastonbury.'

'Yes,' said Harden, as we strolled out of the cathedral. 'What is so important about Glastonbury? Your message said I must not go there without you.'

Holmes halted and faced the Colonel. 'It may be,' he said, 'that you should not go there at all.'

Harden frowned. 'Not go there?' he repeated. 'Why ever not?'

'Colonel,' said my friend, gravely, 'at Winchester you made a bold decision, to stand your ground in the face of Drew's threats – a decision which I applauded. However, the situation has changed. Drew has still not found what he seeks and my information indicates that he intends to be at Glastonbury when you are there. I believe that the heart of Drew's quest lies at Glastonbury and that he is now driven by a real fear that you will discover what he cannot.'

'What of it?' said the Colonel. 'Why should I change my decision?'

'Because,' said Holmes, 'if Drew does not seek to kill you when you arrive in Glastonbury, he will certainly do so before you leave.'

12

ARRIVALS AND DEPARTURES

It was, I suppose, entirely to be expected that no threat would make the old soldier retreat from his position. We left for Glastonbury early on the following day, still accompanied by McMurdo's bodyguard.

Once we had established ourselves at an hotel in the High Street, we walked the short distance to the ruins of the town's abbey, McMurdo's men helping to carry Harden's equipment.

I shall not readily forget my first sight of the sad remains of what was once the greatest shrine in Britain. It was, of course, well into June, and the area around the abbey's remains was a wilderness of weeds and thistles, punctuated here and there by thick clumps of bramble and other bushes that had rooted in the broken walls.

Near to the road stood the intact walls of a graceful chapel, but it was roofless and floored with vegetation. Beyond it, tall splinters of arches reared out of the undergrowth, their graceful, broken curves hinting at the beauty of the intact building. It brought to mind the ruins of Netley Abbey, in which I had often strolled when I studied for the Army Medical Certificate at the hospital nearby, and I reflected on how much of beauty and worth had been destroyed by a greedy and lustful tyrant.

Except where odd footpaths wound through the weeds, the ground underfoot was uneven, made irregular by holes where stones had been dragged out or where concealed fragments of walls still hid in the greenery. As we wandered the area I recalled that somewhere beneath our feet lay the bones of our British saints, David, Patrick, Brigid and Dunstan, probably also the remains of the great King Arthur and perhaps even the remains of Joseph of Arimathea, lost in this rotting wasteland.

Holmes, careful of the Colonel's safety, laid down a plan whereby he and the Colonel moved about with the camera, preceded by two of McMurdo's men, serving both as scouts and to batter down the weeds. The third body-guard and I stayed a little aloof, seeking the nearest eminence to each photographic site and keeping a watch around the whole area.

The sun mounted the sky and the day grew hot. Bees buzzed among the wildflowers that sprang in colourful clumps wherever the ground had been recently disturbed. It became increasingly difficult to maintain an alert watch, but luckily there was no apparent sign of Drew. Apart from an occasional townsman or woman of Glastonbury using the paths through the ruins as a shortcut, we had the old abbey entirely to ourselves.

At last the heat of the day began to slacken. As the sha-dows lengthened, Harden decided that the light was now inadequate for his camera and we made our way back to our hotel. Holmes scanned the register for new arrivals and looked over our fellow guests in the dining-room, but found nothing to cause him concern.

'If this sunshine holds,' said the Colonel, over dinner, 'I think it possible that I shall finish here by tomorrow after-noon.'

'That would be as well,' said Holmes. 'We might even take Drew by surprise and leave before he arrives, though my informer says that we are watched here on Drew's behalf.'

It was not to be. We had finished our meal and removed ourselves to the smoking-room when I realised that I had left my cigarettes in my bedroom. In coming down the stairs from recovering them I saw a small group of men at the registration desk. Foremost among them was a broad-shouldered man with porcine features and a florid complexion.

Some instinct made me believe it was Drew. I stepped back into the shadows on the stairs and pressed close to the banister. The broad man spoke, and the voice was that sinister, diseased croak that Jay Harden had reproduced for us at Winchester.

'Now we know that they are here,' he said, 'we can go back to our friends and make our plans in detail.'

The little group left the hotel's lobby and, as soon as they were out of the door, I hastened to the smoking-room to inform Holmes and the Colonel.

Holmes betrayed no great surprise. 'They have a number of options,' he remarked. 'If they are wise they will wait until the Colonel's work here is done; if they are impetuous they will seek to prevent its completion by an attack tomorrow.'

He turned to Harden. 'It really is most important that your photography is completed tomorrow,' he said. 'I suggest a very early start, as soon as the light is strong enough. Tonight is warm, but I fear I must recommend closed windows and locked doors when we retire. Are you armed, Colonel?'

'There's a brace of derringers in my coat pockets,' Harden replied, 'and two more in my vest. Is that sufficient?'

Holmes smiled. 'I have seen what they can do at short range,' he said. 'What they lack in calibre they make up in surprise, but do remember, Colonel, that this is the West of England, not the Western States. Here the law requires that one is attacked before injuring an enemy.'

The Colonel fixed him with a steady eye. 'If the occasion arises, Mr Holmes,' he said, 'I shall do my best to keep that clear in my mind.'

Although we retired early, each following my friend's advice and locking both doors and windows, it was a long time before I slept. I flung the curtains of the old four-poster bed wide apart so as not to muffle the least

81

sound and, when at last I slept, I did so with one hand firmly grasping my old Adams .450.

In the event the night passed without interruption. We broke our fast early and the High Street was still in shadow when we emerged.

At the abbey ruins the dew still sparkled on the undergrowth and while we waited for sunlight strong enough for the Colonel's purposes Harden amused himself with some dramatic views of the lovely and forlorn remains.

Soon a strong sun was burning down out of a cloudless sky and we adopted the same plan as on the previous day. Now, despite the heat, there was no tendency for our minds to wander. Knowing our adversaries to be somewhere in the town made us all aware that, at any moment, we might find ourselves under an attack of some kind. The rough and overgrown terrain worried my soldier's eye. There were too many places for an ambuscade or an attack from cover. My hand grew moist with grasping the butt of my Adams whenever anything moved within our sight.

By noon the Colonel's work was well advanced and we retreated to the only complete building there, a curious octagonal structure, and made it our stronghold while we refreshed ourselves. Over luncheon Holmes spoke of the long and colourful history of this ancient place, remarking that the very building in which we sat had played host to the ill-fated Duke of Monmouth, two hundred years before, on his way to disaster in the battle of Sedgemoor.

True to his prediction, the Colonel announced the completion of his work in late afternoon, and we withdrew in good order to our hotel. We had ordered tea and were awaiting it in the smoking-room, when the hotel's manager came to us with a telegram for Colonel Harden.

Harden slit open the envelope and his face paled. Wordlessly he passed the flimsy across to Holmes and me. It was dated from London, scarcely an hour before, and ran:

JAY UNWELL STOP NOT SERIOUSLY BUT NEEDS
YOU STOP SO DOES YOUR AFFECTIONATE WIFE
CECILIE

'What will you do?' I asked.

Sherlock Holmes forestalled the reply. 'You must leave
at once, Colonel.' He pulled out his watch. 'You have time
to reach Bristol and a fast train to London. You can be with
your family tonight.'

'But my equipment – my plates!' exclaimed Harden.

'We are engaged to guard not only yourself, but your
experiments, Colonel,' said Holmes. 'Pack as little as you
need and take McMurdo's lads with you. Watson and I
will follow on tomorrow with your equipment.'

He rose and rang the bell, commanding the boy who
responded to see that an overnight bag was packed for the
Colonel at once. Harden capitulated and, once we had
taken our tea, I accompanied him to the railway station.

When I returned to the hotel my friend was in high good
humour. 'Holmes!' I expostulated, 'The boy is sick. That is
hardly a matter for congratulation.'

'Young Jay is a good deal healthier than his father imagines,'
said Holmes, 'and the good Colonel is now safely out of the
way while we try conclusions with Master Drew.'

'Holmes!' I exclaimed. 'You arranged that telegram!
That was unforgivable.'

'My dear Watson, you will have observed that Colonel
Harden is not a man who can be bullied, threatened or
frightened. It was absolutely necessary that there should
be a clear field between us and Drew tonight and the only
way to achieve that was to play upon the Colonel's strong
paternal feelings. In a matter of hours Harden will know
that he has been duped. He will, I suspect, be very angry,
and he has quite sufficient wit to realise who must have
done it In due time I shall have to make my apologies to
him, but for now we must prepare to welcome Mr Drew.'

'What do you mean?' I asked.

'Drew must know that we have finished here, even if he does not know of Harden's departure. Since he has not stopped the Colonel, as we expected he might, he must now seize the results of the Colonel's experiments. I shall spend a little time in the Colonel's room making that easier, after which we shall take a little dinner.'

Over dinner my friend was loquacious on the subject of the ancient Chaldean language and the proper application of the term 'Esquire', but not one word would he address to the business in hand.

We retired early and, as we separated outside the Colonel's erstwhile room, Holmes said, 'You spent a watchful night last night, Watson. I suggest you take your ease tonight. My trap has been set and I would urge you not, in any circumstances, to venture into Harden's room.'

Only Sherlock Holmes could have imagined that such a remark would induce a night of untroubled slumber. Quite unable to repose I sat in my darkened room as the night wore on and all sounds of activity in the hotel ceased.

The faint glimmer of light in my room showed me that it was past two by the clock on the mantelpiece, and my senses were slipping away into sleep when I was jolted awake by the certainty that I had heard a sound in the adjoining room. Now fully alert I listened more intently, but heard nothing for some moments. Then came another sound, more distinct than the first. It was the sound of someone blundering against an item of furniture next door. I recalled Holmes' embargo and satisfied myself that his trap had worked; a burglary was now in progress in the Colonel's room.

To confirm my impression I slipped quietly on to the landing and listened at the Colonel's door. A whispered sussuration reached me through the panel and I was about to turn back to my own room when a further sound stopped me in my tracks. It was the sound of a blow against something soft followed by the strangled groan of an injured man.

In a flash I realised that Holmes was in that room and had come to some harm. I rattled at the ancient doorknob, calling for assistance. Suddenly the door flew open and I sprang into the room.

The chamber was completely dark, save where its one window shed a little light, the less because it was largely blocked by the dark shape of a man. Since I set myself to watch, hours before, my Adams had lain in the pocket of my dressing-gown. Now I whipped it out and fired two shots at the man in the window. I heard a cry, but not such as to suggest a serious injury, and the figure vanished below the sill.

Leaping to the window I leaned out, but the narrow yard below was a pool of blackness in the overcast night and I could not detect any movement. Hastily I turned back to the room.

Now I could see that the curtains of the old-fashioned bed were partly open and a tall figure sprawled between them, its face towards the floor.

Rapidly I lit the bedside candle and as its flame swelled saw, to my utter confusion and dismay, that the figure was that of Colonel Harden and that the back of his silken dressing-gown was darkened by a huge bloodstain.

13

SHERLOCK HOLMES
APOLOGISES

For seconds my astonishment immobilised me, then the trained responses of a medical man took over. I began to lift the injured man back on to the bed. As I did so I was pleased to note that, despite the apparent seriousness of the wound, the Colonel's heart was beating steadily and vigorously.

My shots had aroused the hotel and very shortly an anxious manager with a cluster of staff at his back appeared at the bedroom door. I sent him to my room for my medical bag and asked him to send the remaining staff to their beds.

As I laid my patient face down on the bed, and observed with dismay the huge bloodstain on his dressing-gown, a familiar voice murmured, 'Appearances may be deceptive, Watson. I fancy I shall require only minimal attention.'

'Holmes!' I hissed. 'What on earth have you been doing?'

He chuckled and rolled over, beginning to shrug off the stained dressing-gown. 'I have merely been adding a little spice to my bait for Drew's gang.'

The implications of his conduct struck me and I admit that I became very angry. 'You gave me the most explicit order not to enter this room,' I protested, 'then you disguised yourself as the Colonel and waited for Drew's gang. You must have known you might well have been killed!'

He peeled from his face the moustache and side-whiskers that had emphasised his resemblance to Colonel Harden. 'You have every right to be angry, Watson, but I swear that, when I ordered you not to enter this room, I intended simply to leave an empty room for our enemies to burgle. On consideration I believed that they might see that as a trap and so I capitalised on my appearance. Now Drew will believe that he has not only robbed Harden, but injured or killed him.'

The manager returned with my bag and I took it from him and sent him away. 'Let me see your injuries,' I said to Holmes.

'They are, as I said, minimal. I took the precaution of protecting my back with a couple of the Colonel's plate-carriers held in place with sticking-plaster. The copious blood is of the theatrical variety. You know I never travel without a few little devices.' He rolled over again. 'I think you will find that my worst injury is a nasty little bruise from the edge of a mahogany plate-carrier.'

My examination confirmed his diagnosis and soon his injury was dressed. He sat up on the bed and picked up Harden's dressing-gown. 'I fear,' he remarked, 'that I have ruined the Colonel's dressing-gown.'

'I would have thought,' I replied, 'that when we meet our client again you will have a good deal more to explain than a damaged dressing-gown.'

Holmes laughed outright. 'When we meet the Colonel again,' he said, 'he will have a great deal more to concern him than the demise of his dressing-gown.'

Unconvinced I retired, at last, to my bed. Despite the night's alarums, Holmes was up early in the morning and was already closeted with the hotel's manager when I came down to breakfast. Throughout the morning he was in cheerful and amiable mood while we arranged for our own and the Colonel's luggage to be taken to the railway station and set out for London.

Most of the way to the metropolis my friend treated me to one of his running discourses covering a multiplicity of apparently unrelated subjects, always a sign that he was certain of the progress he was making in an enquiry and was prepared to let his extraordinary intellect run free.

I, by contrast, became increasingly gloomy as London drew nearer and I grew embarrassingly aware of our coming interview with the American Colonel.

We disembarked at Paddington and took a cab into the suburbs where Scotland Yard were guarding the house that held Harden's family. A plain-clothes police officer met us at the door and recognised my friend.

'Come in, sir,' he said. 'Colonel Harden is waiting for you, ever since he saw the afternoon editions.'

I was mystified, but Holmes merely smiled. The officer led us to a study, where the Colonel sat behind a large desk. Without rising, the American waved us to two chairs. When we were seated, he took his cigar from his mouth and looked hard at Holmes.

'There is nothing at all wrong with my son,' he said, emphasising each word, 'and I had it in mind to tell you a few home truths, Mr Holmes. I do not care to be made a monkey of, even by those who believe it is in my best interests.'

Holmes was expressionless. 'Then, Colonel, I can only make the inadequate plea that I acted from the best of motives. I ask your pardon for any distress that I have caused you and will, if you wish to recite them, listen with a good will to any "home truths" you may care to vouchsafe.'

The reply was so unlike my friend that I could only believe that he spoke ironically, but his face remained placidly expressionless.

Harden replaced his cigar and grunted in a slightly mollified fashion. 'I take it that you and my wife arranged the trick with the wire for when you thought things were getting dangerous?' he asked.

'You must not blame Mrs Harden,' said Holmes. 'I had to persuade her very strongly that I must have a means of removing you from the arena if danger became very close, and you would not have left at my request.'

'True,' grunted Harden, 'but why was danger closer then than when we were stumbling about the ruin at Glastonbury under anybody's eyes and guns?'

'At the ruin,' said Holmes, 'we were exposed to attack, but we were a force of six able men, some of us armed. That is, no doubt, why there was no attack. Once your work was complete Drew had even more compelling reasons to attack and the advantage that he knew you would be alone in your hotel room during the hours of darkness. He was almost bound to attack you last night.'

'That didn't worry me,' said the Colonel. 'I mentioned my armament to you, Mr Holmes.'

'So you did,' said Holmes, 'and that increased my determination to remove you from the scene. I could not afford to embroil you in a battle with Drew's men.'

'I would have won,' said Harden, bluntly. 'I killed enough Yankees to train my hand and eye pretty well, and I've killed enough turkeys since to keep well in practice.'

'I do not doubt it, Colonel,' replied Holmes, 'and that was the biggest difficulty of all. Drew, like all his unsavoury kind, is an arrant coward and does not, as a rule, expose himself to the risk of doing his own dirty work. You might have slain a dozen of his henchmen and Drew would still have been on your trail. Besides, it was absolutely essential that Drew believes his plan has succeeded.'

'Succeeded!' ejaculated the Colonel. 'Why the blazes –?'

Holmes interrupted him by reaching for a newspaper that lay on the desk. 'May I ask what interests you here?' he said.

'One of the Scotland Yard men brought it to me. The Stop Press says that the American millionaire John Vincent Harden was seriously injured in a mysterious incident at a Somerset hotel late last night and is in Exeter Infirmary. I wired the hotel and they said you had gone and I was in hospital. I wired the hospital and they said they could not give patients' details by telegraph. I admit that left me pretty nonplussed at first.'

'And then?' said Holmes, raising one eyebrow.

'Then I took a leaf out of your book,' said Harden. 'I thought about it until I realised that you and I had been mistaken for each other before and maybe we had been again.'

'I congratulate you, Colonel,' said Holmes. 'I confess that I encouraged the mistake on this occasion, so that Drew would be the more certain that he had really stolen your exposed plates.'

'My plates!' snapped the Colonel, jerking his cigar away from his mouth. 'What has happened to my plates?'

'Calm yourself, Colonel Harden. When I last saw them, your guardian police officers were unloading them from our cab into the front hall.'

'Then Drew has stolen . . .?'

'. . . a number of boxes clearly marked with your printed labels as exposed and undeveloped plates. They are, however, your reserve supply of unused plates to which I transferred the labels.'

Harden laughed until the tears ran. When he had controlled himself he reached for a decanter and poured us both a large measure of brandy.

As we drank he shook his head slowly. 'So I am dead or dying,' he said, 'and Drew believes that he has whatever it was he is looking for. Mr Holmes, you are a jump ahead of anyone I ever heard of.'

Genuine admiration always warmed my friend and he smiled pleasantly. 'Thank you,' he said, 'but we are only a short jump ahead. Once Drew has those plates developed he will know that he has been tricked. If we are to maintain our lead we must soon know whether the real plates do contain anything of value.'

Harden rose. 'I shall give you dinner,' he announced, 'and afterwards Jay and I will work on my plates until they are done. May I bring my apparatus and my results to your apartment tomorrow at, say, eleven?'

The hour was agreed, we dined well and left the Colonel and Jay to what seemed to be a long night in the photographic laboratory.

Holmes was still in triumphant mood when we arrived back at Baker Street. 'You must remind me,' he said, as we were about to turn in, 'that I have yet to apologise to the Colonel for the destruction of his dressing-gown.'

PICTURES AND PUZZLES

Promptly upon the agreed hour Colonel Harden and his son arrived at Baker Street the next day. They were accompanied by two of their plain-clothes police guard and heavily burdened with cases containing the Colonel's plates and apparatus. With my assistance the load was carried up our seventeen narrow steps and stacked in our sitting-room.

Sherlock Holmes surveyed our cluttered room, now further encumbered with our clients, the police officers and the equipment cases.

'I imagine,' he said to Harden, 'that your device requires a good light.'

'It has its own lamps within it,' responded the Colonel, 'but it will certainly give clearer results in natural sunlight.'

'Then we shall place it where sunlight is available,' said Holmes. 'Watson, be so good as to clear the small table beneath the window.'

The table was cleared and the Colonel's viewing apparatus set upon it. Holmes himself cleared a space at one end of the table where he conducted his chemical experiments. Mrs Hudson was sent for and prevailed upon to serve the police officers refreshments in her own quarters. At last we were able to commence our examination of the Colonel's results.

The viewing apparatus was a mahogany box, some two and a half feet wide, from the front of which projected two lenses set in brass carriers with knurled adjustment screws. Here and there about the box were slots and apertures and each side carried further brass adjustment screws. Harden took a chair in front of the device and held out a hand to his son.

Jay Harden stood by the long boxes of plates. Now he pulled on a pair of wash-leather gloves and selected from the first box a pair of glass plates, passing them to his father.

The Colonel inserted one plate into a slot in each side of the device, applied his eyes to the two lenses and began a series of manipulations of what seemed to be polished reflectors at the rear. Next he turned to the brass knobs, carefully adjusting each in turn. At last he was satisfied and turned to Holmes.

'The apparatus is adjusted for ordinary viewing, Mr Holmes. Would you care to take a look?'

He drew aside his chair and Holmes stooped to peer into the eye-pieces. He was silent for a minute or two, then straightened and said to Harden, 'The effect is extraordinary. Watson, do take a look.'

I have passed many an idle hour with stereoscopes, sometimes with images taken by superior photographers, but none had prepared me for the image that appeared within the Colonel's machine.

Brightly lit by the concentrated sunlight, I saw a black and white reproduction of the ruin at Glastonbury as we had seen it on our first morning. In the foreground a dark clump of brambles emerged from a pool of silvery ground mist and at the rear skeletal fragments of arches reared out of the undergrowth into the morning sun. I could see that the photographic images were being reflected into two mirrors, which seemed to give them a greater depth and luminescence than the ordinary card-mounted print.

I sat back with an exclamation of surprise and delight. 'Look again, doctor,' said the Colonel and reached for one of the brass knobs.

I reapplied my eyes to the lenses and watched in amazement as the scene before me shifted in response to the Colonel's manipulations. The clump of brambles moved and swelled until it grew blurred, as though it were right at the forward edge of my visual field; the mist spread and widened and the stone arches drew apart as I watched. When the images stopped moving it was as though I had stepped several feet forward from the original viewpoint.

Holmes took his turn at the lenses and, like me, was astounded by the magical effects that the machine manifested.

'If your adjustments can be calibrated and standardised,' he told Harden, 'you will have taken photography in a new and immensely useful direction. It will become more than an easy technique for recording visual information – it will be a wonderfully flexible tool for the analysis of that information.'

Harden gave him a brief nod of acknowledgement. 'Thank you,' he said. 'It would please me mightily if that is where my work ends. Now you have seen what my little device can do, can you give me any indication as to how we can use it to analyse my pictures from Glastonbury?'

Holmes sat at the dining-table. 'Let us consider what few facts we have,' he said. 'Firstly, Moriarty discovered by some means that something he considered desirable was to be sought for at Glastonbury.' He struck his points off on his long fingers. 'Secondly, Porlock and the British Museum have told us that King Henry also sought it and failed. Thirdly, Drew, on learning of your intended experiments at Glastonbury, was immediately concerned to drive you away. Fourthly, when his efforts failed, he attempted to seize your plates.'

He paused and looked around at us, as though he had made his meaning quite clear.

'Sure enough,' said the Colonel, 'but how do those facts tell us what to look for?'

'That Moriarty and Drew and, indeed, King Henry have sought this item indicates either that it is very valuable or that it confers some power or privilege upon its holder. The nickname "the Devil's Grail" suggests the latter. The King's failure to find it makes it clear that it was concealed before 1539 when he ordered the looting of Glastonbury.

From whatever source we know not, Drew has developed the idea that your plates will reveal the thing itself or clues to its whereabouts. Is it not, therefore, obvious that we are seeking something that has been a part of the abbey for at least three and a half centuries and that was concealed from Henry's searchers? And is it not equally clear that Drew is certain that it still exists and that it can be seen in your photographs?'

He emphasised each of the last four words, then he rose and searched quickly among the pigeon-holes of his desk. Seizing a slip of paper he resumed his seat by the table.

'We are, I think, agreed that we are dealing with some mystery of a perverse religious cult. In the course of my researches at the British Museum I came upon a passage in a twelfth-century writer that hints at some religious mystery hidden at Glastonbury, but available to those who understood.'

He read from the paper:

> 'The very floor is inlaid with polished stones. The sides of the altar and the altar itself, above and below, are laden with many relics. Furthermore, there may be seen, in all parts of the pavement, stones purposely placed in interlaced triangles and squares, sealed with lead. If I believe a sacred mystery to be concealed beneath them I do no harm to religion.

'The writer of that strange description was one William of Malmesbury, a priest himself, who knew Glastonbury well. He studied in its great library. If he believed that religious mysteries were concealed by meaningful patterns in the very floor of the abbey, we should take his evidence seriously.'

'Are you suggesting,' I asked, 'that whatever secret Drew is seeking is the same that this William referred to six hundred years ago?'

'It might be,' said my friend, 'and if it is then we and Drew are defeated, for the Colonel will confirm that no part of that patterned floor around the altar still survives. However, I noted the passage merely as evidence that a practice existed, three centuries before Henry the Eighth, of concealing religious mysteries by a pattern whose significance was evident only to the initiate. If I am correct in that surmise, then Drew may be right and we may be able to unearth some surviving clue.'

'Now I understand,' said Harden, 'why you asked me to concentrate on certain decorations. Shall we begin with them?'

'I think a mixture of the plates which I requested and any of your own which may reveal any apparently decorative pattern should provide the best chance,' said Holmes.

So the work began. Holmes and the Colonel applied themselves to the machine while Jay stood by, serving them with the plates they required and returning unwanted ones to their slotted container. Each plate remained in the device for many minutes as both researchers scanned it and readjusted the many screws on the machine. Occasionally Holmes would invite me to comment on a specimen which they were viewing, but I cannot record that I was of much assistance. I saw many fine photographs of details of carvings, but none revealed any pattern to my mind. I began to wonder if Holmes had not misled himself.

Time and again the reflectors were adjusted to take account of the sun's position, but in the end it had passed so far over the street as to make further use of its light impossible.

'What of your lamps?' Holmes asked the Colonel.

'I can light them,' said Harden, 'but I don't believe they will give you the degree of detail you require.'

'Very well,' said Holmes, 'then we must abandon our labours and permit Mrs Hudson to serve us a belated luncheon. We have, at the least, reduced the possibilities to a half-dozen plates,' and he gestured to a small pile that had not been returned to their containers.

We did little justice to Mrs Hudson's cooking, eating largely in silence, and an atmosphere of frustration, if not of failure, burdened our little group. While the Colonel smoked after the meal, Holmes rose and stepped to the window. He took his large hand lens and began taking plates from the small pile, holding each up against the window and examining it closely with his glass.

As we rose from the table he spoke over his shoulder. 'Colonel Harden,' he said, 'is there any reason why you cannot make an enlarged print upon paper from one of these plates?'

'Why, no,' said Harden, 'that would be no problem. I can only, of course, print the actual image on the glass, not any of the variations I can produce in my apparatus, but if that is helpful to you I could make one in minutes.'

Holmes turned and handed Jay a plate. 'I would like', he said, 'the largest possible print of this plate. If it could be manufactured and delivered to me this evening I would esteem it a particular favour.'

'You shall have it, Mr Holmes,' asserted the Colonel. Within minutes the equipment had been packed away, the police officers summoned and the boxes hauled downstairs. We agreed to meet again at eleven in the morning, and father and son took their leave.

With our guests gone, Holmes flung himself at length upon the sofa, lit his pipe and retreated into silence. I had learned not to interrupt him in this state and passed a dull afternoon with magazines. In due course Mrs Hudson brought our tea, but my friend could not be persuaded to come to the table, continuing to stare at the wall and smoke furiously. The meal had been cleared away when a messenger arrived from the Colonel, bringing a print of the plate, some two feet square.

Holmes arose at last and laid the still-moist print upon the dining-table. Now I could see that it showed a section of richly decorated tiling, rendered in crystal clarity in the Colonel's picture.

'Wonderful!' breathed Holmes, smoothing the print out upon the velvet cloth. 'Now I have something to work upon.'

His response to the picture led me to hope that he might now become more communicative, but I was to be disappointed. The evening passed as the afternoon, save that Holmes now sat hunched at the table, his pipe firmly gripped in his teeth, poring over the photograph with his hand lens.

At length I decided to take an early night. Holmes took sufficient notice of my going to enquire, 'Before you turn in, Watson, have you any small change on you?'

Shaking my head in puzzlement at his extraordinary question, I thrust a hand into my pocket and drew out a handful of coins.

Holmes cast his eye over them. 'A half-crown, a penny and a sixpence should be sufficient,' he remarked, and selected the coins from my outstretched hand. 'Thank you, Watson. Good-night.'

I turned briefly at the door to see him hunched once again over the enlarged photograph.

15

WHEELS WITHIN WHEELS

I was not greatly surprised, when I rose the next morning, to find that the sitting-room was grey with pipe smoke and that Holmes still sat by the dining-table. He showed no sign of having left his post all night, but the table was now littered with a drift of paper, each sheet bearing a pencilled pattern of concentric circles. Harden's photograph hung from the mantelpiece, transfixed by one leg of a pair of dividers.

'Faugh!' I exclaimed, as I made my way through the fug to open the window. 'Surely you have not been staring at that photograph all night, Holmes?'

His eyes, which had been half closed, snapped open. 'Good morning, Watson,' he said. 'I have been attempting to rationalise an instinctive response.'

'Really?' I said. 'I would not have thought that you placed any trust in instinctive responses.'

'On the contrary,' he said, 'I have trained myself for many years in the hope that certain abilities derived from rationalisation and honed by practice might become instinctive. It may be that I have succeeded too well.'

'In what way?' I asked, taking a seat by the cluttered table.

He pointed to the enlarged photograph. 'What do you make of that?' he asked.

The picture showed an area of square earthenware tiles, each bearing a pattern. The tiles were laid in an array of about twelve across by fourteen down, though many were broken or entirely missing. The centre of each tile bore an eight-pointed star, the interstices of which contained eight small six-pointed stars, and this pattern was enclosed within three concentric circles. The decoration was contrived in such a fashion that the circles of each tile

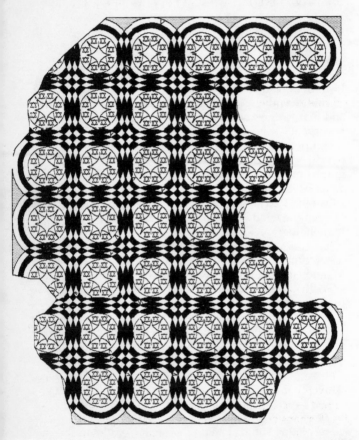

A portion of the Glastonbury pattern, drawn from John V. Harden's Stereoscopic Photographs.

appeared to overlap with its neighbours, forming ornamental crosses where four tiles came together. (Figure 1 depicts a diagram drawn from the photograph.)

'I cannot say,' I answered, after peering at the picture for some time. 'Having regard to where it was found, it may well be that the pattern contains all manner of religious symbols, but I could not begin to interpret them.'

'As to that,' said Holmes, 'the eight-pointed stars may indicate the Virgin Mary, who is sometimes known as the Star of Heaven; the smaller stars are each versions of Solomon's Star, symbolic of the union of heaven above and the earth below; the three circles may signify the layers of the old Celtic spherical cosmos and the repeated overlapping of them repeats the sign of the Cross, but all of that is obvious. They were not the reason that I asked Harden to photograph this pattern.'

'Then what was?' I enquired.

'An uneasy and perhaps irrational belief that this florid pattern conceals a second, more subtle, design. I have refined my habits of observation and ratiocination to such an extent that I may have detected some underlying pattern instinctively which now refuses to reveal itself to the conscious brain.'

He lifted a few of the pencil drawings that littered the table. 'I have examined this pattern through every variation of Colonel Harden's singular machine, I have applied my lens to the original plates, and, with the assistance of your pocket change, I have drawn diagrams of it. I have examined and charted every variation in the pattern, whether deliberate or accidental, down to the very slips of the graver that incised the ornaments, yet its secret, if it has one, does not reveal itself to me.'

'Perhaps,' I ventured, 'you are right, and you have allowed your instincts to mislead you.'

I had expected an angry refutation, but he sighed wearily. 'Perhaps you are right, Watson. Perhaps you are right,' and bundling his papers together he removed them to his experimental bench as Mrs Hudson entered to serve breakfast.

Once again we took our meal in silence. Holmes barely ate at all, consuming several cups of strong coffee. When breakfast had been cleared away he asked Mrs Hudson for another pot of coffee and took himself and his papers to the table beneath the window, where he alternated between drawing circles around coins and staring out of the window while his long fingers drummed on the table.

I had occupied myself with the morning papers for some time when it occurred to me that we had a further appointment with Colonel Harden. A glance at the mantel-piece clock revealed an entirely unlikely time, and a check with my watch showed that our timepiece was, as often, running slow. I stepped across to the fireplace and shook the offending instrument.

'It is a great pity,' I complained aloud, 'that our age of machine tools and elaborate engineering cannot produce a sitting-room clock as reliable as the clock at Wells.'

Holmes turned a blank face to me. 'The clock at Wells?' he repeated. 'What are you ...? The clock at Wells! Watson, you are right! The circles of the cosmos, the rotating stars! Once again you have pointed me in the right direction.'

He took one of his diagrams and began to scribble on it, his face beaming with pleasure, while I stood by complete-ly bewildered. He was still scribbling when Mrs Hudson entered to announce the arrival of the Hardens. Holmes rose to meet them with his sheet of paper in his hand.

'Come in, come in!' he cried. 'I believe that I have news for you. Jay, be so kind as to detach your father's photo-graph from the mantelpiece.'

The boy sprang to do Holmes' bidding and, when we were all seated, my friend laid the picture on the dining-table once more and pointed to a corner of the pattern with a long finger.

'Observe,' he said, 'that each part of the pattern consists of three concentric circles with an eight-pointed star at their centre. Imagine, if you will, that the points of the star are extended to the perimeter of the outer circle. What do we have?'

We all looked at him, blankly.

'In each case you have a circular figure, divided into thirty-two segments,' he continued, impatiently. 'Now, the central ornament does not, at any point, overlap with its neighbours, but all of the three outer circles do so; they create a richly confused pattern, the obvious element of which is a repeating pattern of crosses where four sets of circles are laid over each other.'

'I had imagined the crosses to be the reason for the pattern,' observed the Colonel.

'As you were intended to do,' said Holmes. 'Any casual eye coming to rest on this decoration, in its religious setting, would perceive the repeating array of crosses and linger on them, or on the decoration at the heart of each circle, taking them to be mystical symbols used as decoration.'

'And what are they, Mr Holmes?' asked Jay.

'Distractions,' replied my friend. 'The maker's real purpose lies hidden in the overlapping rings.'

'But each set is identical,' I protested. 'The pattern of overlaps is the same at every junction.'

'To a superficial eye, yes,' said Holmes, and laid his hand lens on the photograph.

Jay took up the instrument and scanned a part of the photograph earnestly. After a moment he looked up. 'Dr Watson is right,' he said. 'There is no difference between the sets of circles.'

'Look again, young man,' said Holmes, taking his pipe from his pocket. 'With the aid of the lens you should be able to see a series of tiny marks in each set of circles.'

Jay reapplied the lens, and we waited. At length he looked up again. 'There are marks there,' he said, slowly, 'but they look like tool marks.'

'Precisely,' said Holmes, applying a match to his pipe. 'Go back, if you will, to the figure I asked you to imagine, and erase the centre to leave only the three circles. What then do you have?'

'Three circles divided into twenty-four parts,' said the boy promptly, but he was frowning in puzzlement.

'Then,' said Holmes, 'if you have row upon row of such figures – as we have here – it becomes possible to distinguish two dozen separate patterns by marking one of the segments.'

I recalled some of my friend's earlier dissertations on codes and ciphers and a flicker of illumination reached me, but I saw an objection.

'But the alphabet,' I protested, 'has twenty-six letters.'

'That has not always been the case,' said Holmes. 'It has had twenty-two, twenty-three, twenty-four and twenty-five letters on occasion. It is common to find old alphabets where I and J are interchangeable, or V and W, and the Celtic alphabet had neither a Q nor a Z.'

'Then you believe that each of these circular decorations indicates a letter?' asked Colonel Harden.

'I had reached that conclusion just as you arrived,' said Holmes. 'I have not yet put it to the test.'

'But the marks in the circles are only tiny marks of a tool-point,' protested the younger Harden.

'What more natural?' asked Holmes. 'The pattern is constructed partly by cutting designs in wet clay. How very reasonable that it should contain what appear to be the marks of minor errors with a cutting or graving tool.'

We all looked at him in silence. 'Come,' he said. 'Let us put our theory into practice and see if we can unlock the secrets of this fragment.'

16

THE GLASTONBURY FRAGMENT

Holmes laid a fresh sheet of paper on the table and, with firm strokes, laid out a pattern of twelve squares by fourteen.

'This will serve,' he announced, 'as a diagram of the pattern. If I am right it should now be a relatively simple task to transfer on to it our discoveries from the photograph.'

'But how can you determine which mark indicates which letter?' I asked.

'By trial and error, Watson; but there should not be many errors. This cunning pattern is reminiscent of a cipher originated by the Brotherhood of the Rosy Cross and still used among Freemasons. Their version is simpler, employing a series of separate circles. Our devious old monk has made the matter more complex by overlaying three circles into one pattern, but I believe we shall get the better of him.'

'What language is this likely to be in?' asked Harden. 'What did they speak at Glastonbury in olden times?'

'To be sure of that,' said Holmes, 'we would need to know exactly when this was constructed. The abbey was built in the early twelfth century, burned down and was rebuilt later in the century. We do not know if this fragment is from the earlier or the later building, but we do know it pre-dates the Reformation. Even so it may have been constructed at any time between the early twelfth century and the middle of the sixteenth. Its language will be monkish Latin, Old English or possibly Old Gaelic or

Welsh, perhaps Norman French. Fortunately I have an acquaintance with them all.'

He turned back to the photograph and began to pencil letters on his diagram.

'First we have a missing tile,' he said, 'then four letters, then the remainder of the row is gone. The surviving symbols appear to be C, C, L and E.'

'A Roman date followed by a word beginning with E?' I suggested.

'Possibly,' he murmured, and carried on writing. 'In the second row we have U, S, Z, D, Z, R – this is nonsense!' he exclaimed. 'Even the Slavic languages contain no such combination.'

'I thought you said that the Celts had no Z,' said Jay Harden.

'True,' said Holmes, 'and if Watson is right and this is Latin then the U and S in the second line may be a Latin word ending. If he used an alphabet of twenty-three letters, he may have used his twenty-fourth symbol as punctuation. That would give us this,' and he scribbled quickly at the edge of his diagram:

```
–  C  C  L  E  –  –  –  –  – –  –
U  S  *  D  *  R  *  –  –  O  M  –
```

'Were ancient monks really skilled in this kind of thing?' I asked. 'Surely such a complicated code would be relatively modern.'

'Watson, Watson,' sighed Holmes, shaking his head, 'sometimes I believe a classical education was wasted on you. It is probable that secret messages were devised very shortly after the invention of writing. Thucydides tells us that the Spartans had a device known as a skytale to assist them in creating coded messages. I have thought sometimes of devoting a monograph to those forgotten occasions when a secret message has diverted the course of history, as when Perceval deciphered the Spanish documents that warned us of the coming of the Armada.'

'I had thought only that monks devoted their time to things of the spirit,' I said.

'Some monks, Watson,' said Holmes. 'Some were notorious for their devotion to the flesh and others had minds that could devise a clock that would run for five hundred years.'

Jay Harden interrupted us. 'Excuse me, Mr Holmes, but I think I know what this is,' he said, indicating Holmes' marginal note. 'I don't think it's a date. I think this top word is Ecclesiasticus.'

Holmes' eyes followed the boy's pointing finger. 'You may very well be correct,' he said. 'There is a Bible somewhere in the shelves behind you, if you would care to check the reference.'

'But what chapter and verse will it be?' I enquired.

'D and R,' replied Holmes, pointing. 'The fourth and seventeenth letters of our twenty-three letter alphabet.'

Jay had found the Bible and was thumbing through it. Now he returned to the table. 'The Book of Ecclesiastes, fourth chapter, seventeenth verse,' he announced, then read aloud the following verse:

> 'For at the first she will walk with him by crooked ways, and bring fear and dread upon him, and torment him with her discipline until she may trust his soul, and try him by her laws. Then she will return the straight way unto him and comfort him and show him her secrets.'

Holmes smiled broadly. 'Well done, Jay,' he said. 'We could not have a clearer proof that we are on the right track. It cannot be chance that the passage relates to a female who rules by fear and conceals her secrets. The biblical introduction has also the virtue that it would discourage any enquirer who unravelled the pattern thus far. It gives the impression that all the panel contains are concealed quotations. What a marvellously cunning man was our old monk!'

He picked up one of his sheets of concentric circles and jotted on it. 'There,' he said, when he had finished, 'I have constructed a quick clue to the pattern. Now you can see at a glance how the pattern runs.'

I examined the paper and saw that he had drawn in a V-shaped mark on each set of circles. In the first eight circles the position of the mark rotated around the eight sectors of

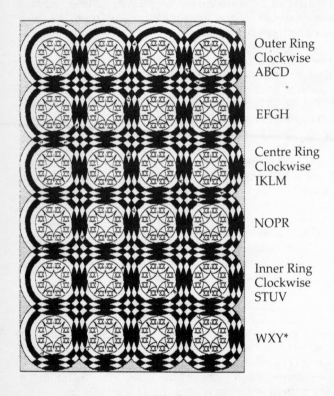

Outer Ring
Clockwise
ABCD

EFGH

Centre Ring
Clockwise
IKLM

NOPR

Inner Ring
Clockwise
STUV

WXY*

The Glastonbury Fragment
The clue that Holmes constructed, showing how letters can be derived from the pattern.

the outer circle, representing the letters A to H; in the next eight the marks ran around the middle circle, representing the letters I to R, with no J and no Q, and in the inner circle they stood for the letters S to Y with a full stop in the twenty-fourth segment. (A more elaborate version of his diagram appears in Figure 2.)

'Remarkable, Holmes,' I said, 'but here you have drawn each set of circles separately. The real pattern overlaps and surely there will be occasions when more than one mark appears in one ring?'

'Very astute of you, Watson,' replied Holmes, 'but that is one of the reasons why the mark is that of a pointed tool. Each marker is pointed towards the circle to which it belongs.'

Taking his clue in one hand, he quickly filled in letters on the squared paper, until he had the following:

```
E   C   C   L   E   S   I   A   S   T   I   C
U   S   *   4   *   17  *           T   O   M
    N   G   I   N   G   S   T   O   N   E   P
    S   E   Y   E   G   R   E   A   T   E
    A   S   T   E   T   O   T   H       E
    N   G   E   S   *   A   T   T   E   G
O   R   S   E   G   R   A   V   E   L   O   K
E   T   O   Y   E   G   R   A   V   E   O   F
    U   R   S   S   O   N   N   E
*   H   A   L   F   E   W   A   Y   E   T
Y   E   R   I   N       D   W   E   L
    I   T   T   L   Y   E   S   T   W
R   M   E   S   S   P   A   N   N   E   D   E
E   P   *   C   U   R   S   E   D       E
```

Colonel Harden had watched in silence. Now he read Holmes' diagram and said, 'How in blazes did you hit on this one pattern in all that mess of ruins, Mr Holmes?'

'The recognition of patterns, or their absence, is a fundamental part of any analysis, whether scientific or historical,' said Holmes. 'I always approach a problem by seeking any patterns that the data may reveal or seeking to explain any pattern that should be present but which is absent or broken. With William of Malmesbury in mind I looked for any pattern that might carry information and struck upon this one because there seemed to be some suggestion of a secondary rhythm underlying the more obvious decoration.'

'Wonderful!' said Harden. 'And it is in Old English.'

'Indeed,' said Holmes, 'which is not what I had expected, but it makes it easier to fill in some of the missing letters by inspection, since we have a number of words which are clearly complete.'

I had been examining my friend's results. 'I can see STONE and EYE and probably HASTE,' I remarked, 'and the name SEGRAVE and FEW and ERIN, YES and MESS and PANNED.'

'Well done, Watson,' remarked Holmes. 'Unhappily only one of those words appears in the message.'

'Apart from HASTE, the others are plainly there,' I protested.

'It is an error of the greatest dimension to attempt to analyse parts of a puzzle in isolation from the structure of the problem as a whole,' said Holmes. 'Pray consider this,' and he wrote a few quick lines and laid them in the centre of the table. He had altered the spacing of the message, as below:

ECCLESIASTICUS, 4,17.– –OMHANGINGSTONE
PASSE YE GREATE WASTE TO THREE
– – NGES* ATTE GORSE GRAVE LOKE
TO YE GRAVE OF – – – – URS SONNE*
HALFEWAYE TO YE RIN – – D WELL –
IT LYES TWO ARMES SPANNE DEEPE
* CURSED BE . . .

'You have written in more letters,' I said, 'but I grant you it makes a lot more sense.'

'And, as always, the more that you can add, the more that reveals itself. The first word of the message is evidently FROM, since there is a TO later in the same phrase, and

110

The Glastonbury Fragment

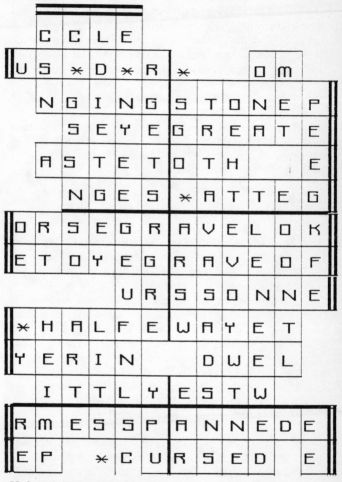

Holmes' diagram showing the letters he derived from the Glastonbury Fragment.

the second grave must surely be of ARTHUR'S son, since this pattern was set up only a few feet from Arthur's grave.'

'What? The king, Arthur?' exclaimed Jay Harden, his eyes wide.

'If you were British, my boy,' said Holmes, with mock gravity, 'you would know that there has only ever been one Arthur of consequence, and he was buried in front of Glastonbury Abbey's altar.'

'Do we have the whole message now?' asked the Colonel.

'Not quite,' said Sherlock Holmes. 'There are two phrases that puzzle me slightly,' and he ran a pencilled loop around each:

    TO THREE – – NGES

    YE RIN – – D WELL –

'The last character in the second phrase is, I believe, either an E or a stop and need not concern us for WELLE or WELL are the same word, but what are the other four characters?'

'Hinges or ranges?' I hazarded.

'You are misled by the old-fashioned E,' said Holmes. 'It is more likely a word that no longer has a final E, such as king or ring. Is there a place called Three Kings?'

No one could recall one and at last Jay suggested, 'Mightn't it be rings, Mr Holmes? There are three rings in each piece of the pattern. Is that a clue?'

'You may be right,' mused Holmes, 'and your suggestion has the virtue that it would fit with the second phrase.' He wrote again, then presented this:

ECCLESIASTICUS, 4, 17. FROM HANGING STONE PASS THE GREAT WASTE TO THREE RINGS. AT GORSE GRAVE LOOK TO THE GRAVE OF ARTHUR'S SON. HALFWAY TO THE RINGED WELL IT LIES TWO ARMS SPAN DEEP.

112

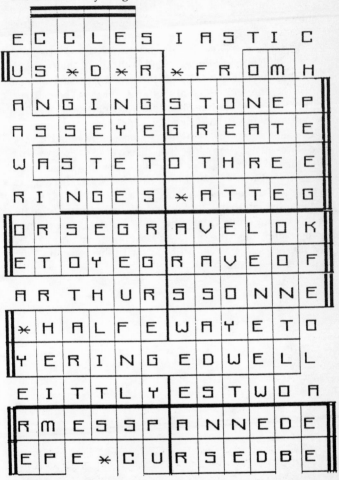

E	C	C	L	E	S		I	A	S	T	I	C
U	S	*	D	*	R		*	F	R	O	M	H
A	N	G	I	N	G		S	T	O	N	E	P
A	S	S	E	Y	E		G	R	E	A	T	E
W	A	S	T	E	T	O		T	H	R	E	E
R	I	N	G	E	S		*	A	T	T	E	G
O	R	S	E	G	R	A	V	E	L	O	K
E	T	O	Y	E	G	R	A	V	E	O	F
A	R	T	H	U	R	S		S	O	N	N	E
*	H	A	L	F	E		W	A	Y	E	T	O
Y	E	R	I	N	G		E	D	W	E	L	L
E	I	T	T	L	Y		E	S	T	W	O	A
R	M	E	S	S	P	A	N	N	E	D	E
E	P	E	*	C	U	R	S	E	D	B	E

Holmes' completed diagram with the missing letters inserted

Each of us examined it in turn. The Colonel was last and when he had seen the note he handed it back to Holmes. 'If I had not seen you do it, Mr Holmes, I shouldn't have believed what you have done this morning. I will allow that when we left here yesterday I was beginning to believe you were barking up a completely wrong tree.'

Sherlock Holmes laughed. 'And I will allow,' he rejoined, 'that there were times last night when I might have agreed with you. Nevertheless, only half the work has been done, and it may prove to have been the easy half.'

'Why do you say so?' asked Harden.

'Oh, if our reading is right, we have unravelled a very accurate instruction for the discovery of something buried, and in the light of what we know that can only be Moriarty's Devil's Grail, but we have now to discover in what district these markers lie.'

We must all have looked crestfallen, for my friend laughed suddenly. 'Come,' he said, 'at least the next stage is an exercise for the mind and the memory and can be readily carried out over luncheon with the assistance of a bottle of something!'

17

THE SEARCH
FOR ARTHUR'S SON

The morning's success had transfigured Holmes and, over luncheon, he was a charming companion and host, so that we did not turn our minds to solving our conundrum until the table was cleared and cigarettes and pipes lighted.

'Now, gentlemen,' he said at last, drawing the slip of paper bearing his translation from his pocket, 'we have a biblical reference that certifies that we are on the right track, and beyond that a series of instructions which are certainly correct in many parts but which may enshrine our errors in others.'

He laid the paper on the table. 'If our version is accurate,' he said, 'then we have precise directions as to the location of the Devil's Grail, but we know not where they begin nor where they end. Indeed, so old is this riddle that the markers may not still exist.'

'How do we proceed?' I enquired.

'Find the hanging stone?' suggested Jay.

'That is easier said than done,' said Holmes. 'It may refer to a natural formation such as the Logan Stone in Cornwall or the Buck Stone in the Forest of Dean, but it may equally refer to one of the many thousands of ancient stones that our ancestors erected all over these islands.'

'Might it not be one of the stones you have mentioned?' said the Colonel.

'I doubt that it is the Buck Stone,' said Holmes, 'because it stands in an ancient forest and there is no great waste nearby.'

'The Logan Stone has moors at hand – they might be the great waste,' I said; 'and there are Stone Age monuments and circles in the vicinity.'

'True' said Holmes, 'but where, in that district, is the grave of Arthur's son?'

'Is it not said', I asked, 'that the name of Stonehenge means "the hanging stones"?'

'A good thought, Watson. Let us consider it,' said my friend. 'We must find a great waste, three rings, a grave of Arthur's son and a ringed well, whatever that may be. Are there such in the vicinity of Stonehenge?'

'I would surmise that Salisbury Plain is the great waste,' said the Colonel.

Holmes left the table to find a map and returned to spread it before us.

'We have a hanging stone and a great waste,' he said, laying his finger on Stonehenge, 'and beyond the great waste we have Avebury, another ancient temple which, in its day, displayed three rings of stone.'

The Colonel, Jay and I exchanged pleased expressions while my friend's finger roamed over the map.

'Where,' he asked at last, 'is the grave of Arthur's son?'

'There are a great many burial mounds around Stonehenge,' said the Colonel.

'I grant you,' said Holmes, 'but which one covers Arthur's son? Gerald of Monmouth, who wrote in the same century when Glastonbury Abbey was burned and rebuilt, tells us that Uther and Ambrosius, Arthur's father and uncle, were buried at Stonehenge. He devotes a long passage to the discovery of Arthur's own grave at Glastonbury, but he never mentions a grave of Arthur's son.'

'I did not know that King Arthur had a son,' remarked Jay.

'He had several,' said Holmes, 'if the ancient stories can be believed. There was a little Arthur, but there were also Llachau, Loholt, Borre, Rowland, Gwydre, Amr, Adeluf, Ilinot, Morgan the Black and Patrick the Red,' and he counted them off on his fingers. 'Even Mordred, who brought about the ruin of Arthur's kingdom, is said by some to have been a son of the King.'

'Could it be Mordred's grave?' I enquired.

'It could, Watson, it could. And heaven help us if it is!' exclaimed Holmes.

'Why so?' I asked.

'Because,' said Holmes, 'Mordred was slain in the great final battle at Camlan and, one imagines, buried there.'

'Then we must find the battlefield,' I said. 'Surely its location is known?'

Holmes laughed. 'Its location is too well known – and always in a different place. It is at Camelford or at Camborne in Cornwall, it is at Camlann in Wales, it is at Colchester in Essex. Indeed, if Tennyson is right then it may never be found.'

'Why not, Mr Holmes?' asked young Harden.

' "So all day long the noise of battle rolled among the mountains by the winter sea," ' quoted Holmes, ' "till all King Arthur's table, man by man, lay fallen in Lyonesse about their lord, King Arthur." '

'Where is Lyonesse?' asked the boy.

'Beyond Land's End, beneath the waters of the Atlantic Ocean,' said Holmes.

'Then a stone in Cornwall might be a pointer to it?' said Jay, and his face fell as he realised what that implied.

'I suggest,' said Holmes, 'that we are approaching the problem from the wrong point. Britain is littered with hanging stones and wells. If the rings are ancient stone circles, then there are hundreds of them, scattered from the northernmost parts of Scotland, through Wales and all the western part of England. We must take the most exclusive marker – the grave of Arthur's son.'

'But you said that there is no such grave,' I complained.

'You misremember, Watson. I said only that there is no such grave known at Stonehenge or at the Logan Stone. There may well be one elsewhere.'

Colonel Harden had been sitting back from the table, frowning in concentration. After a moment he leaned

117

forward and said, 'If I recall aright, Arthur killed another of his sons.'

'Are you not thinking of Llachau, who was killed by Sir Kay?' asked Holmes.

'I don't think so,' said the Colonel. 'I've been preparing for this trip for some time, and I've done a deal of reading about your antiquities. Now somewhere I seem to have read about Arthur killing one of his sons and burying him in a mound that keeps changing its size. It was in one of the ancient writers.'

Holmes rose and stepped to the bookcase. 'It is not Geoffrey,' he said. 'Gildas hated Arthur and ignored him.' He stroked his chin thoughtfully. 'Not Giraldus, which I reread recently. Was it Nennius?'

'Certainly I read Nennius,' said Harden, 'but I can't be sure.'

Holmes pulled a volume down and began to skim through it. At last he turned back to the table, bringing the book with him.

'Your memory does you credit, Colonel,' he said, and running his finger across the page he translated from the Latin text:

'This is where Arthur the warrior slew his son Amr and buried him by a spring in Ercing, and when men come to measure the mound it is sometimes seven feet in length, sometimes fifteen feet and sometimes nine, and I have seen this.'

'Where on earth is Ercing?' I asked.

'That I can tell you,' said Holmes. 'My researches into ancient charters have made me familiar with the old boundaries. Ercing was once a kingdom that lay between the Monnow and the Wye in what is now Herefordshire.'

'What about the well and all that?' asked Jay.

'Nennius says that Amr was buried by a spring,' said Holmes. 'We appear to have two of the markers we

sought. Now we must go and inspect the ground ourselves.'

'Go to Herefordshire?' I exclaimed.

'Of course,' said Holmes. 'We have passed a pleasant
day in parlour word games and history tests, but we must
not forget that my ruse to delay Drew will have lasted no
longer than it took him to have the substitute plates
developed. By now that has occurred and he will be seeking to wrest from us the original plates or the knowledge
we have gained from them. He knows now that he failed
to kill Colonel Harden at Glastonbury. We must be on the
way before he makes another attempt.'

18

A DESPERATE STRATAGEM

Once my friend had made up his mind to action he was not one to waste time. In a very short time our bags were packed and we set out for the Hardens' retreat, to return young Jay to his mother. The Colonel wired ahead for his bags to be prepared and it was intended that we should set out for Herefordshire that evening.

The June day was warm, but it had darkened and become overcast and rain threatened as our carriage turned southwards out of the city. Our driver was, of course, one of the officers assigned to the Colonel's family, and another, Sergeant Turley, rode with us in the carriage.

I recall that the journey to the Colonel's home should have taken a little over an hour and we proposed to go from there to a suburban railway station where we would take a connection for the main line.

There is little more depressing than to pass through the suburban districts of London. The miles of streets that have, in recent years, grown like a fungus around the city have little to stimulate the imagination, and once our journey was well under way all conversation among our small party ceased. The rain began and became steady and it was the more to our surprise that, after approximately a half-hour, our driver slowed to a halt at the lower end of a long, curving crescent. We felt the conveyance rock as our driver climbed down from his box.

Sergeant Turley got out and went to his colleague, but he returned after a moment.

'I beg your pardon, Mr Holmes, but I think you should have a word with Constable Evans.'

Holmes stepped out and I leaned from the window. Our driver was crouched beside the off-side front wheel, ostensibly examining its hub. I heard the conversation that passed.

'What seems to be the trouble?' asked Holmes.

'There's nothing wrong with the wheel, sir,' said Evans. 'I'm just making out as there might be so no one can see as I stopped deliberate.'

'Then what has stopped us?' said Holmes.

'When we left Baker Street,' said the constable, 'I thought a hansom pulled off by Tussaud's, but I wasn't sure. But there's been one following us ever since, sir.'

'Are you sure?' demanded Holmes.

'I wasn't at first, sir, because of all the other traffic, but since we got out of the main streets I've been more and more certain. He hangs back, sir, and only comes into a road well after us, but he's on our heels all right.'

Holmes stepped to the window. 'Do you hear, Watson?' he asked, while his eyes scanned the crescent behind us.

'Yes,' I replied. 'The constable seems sure. What shall we do?'

'It was a team of three that Drew sent to watch the Hardens in Winchester,' mused Holmes. 'A hansom will not easily carry more. There will be a driver, someone to direct affairs, and a man to walk ahead at each turn to observe our movements. It is unlikely that there are more, whereas we are six.'

'Do you propose an ambush?' I asked.

'No, Watson,' said Holmes. 'I would not shock the sensibilities of this crescent's occupants by subjecting it to fisticuffs or gunplay. I think we can be more subtle than that.'

He turned back to the driver. 'Start up again and take it slow and steady,' he commanded briskly. 'Keep looking to that wheel as though you were uncertain of it. Turn right at the bottom of the crescent. When you reach the main road, turn left for the railway station and pull as close to the entrance as you can. Knock twice on the roof as we arrive there.'

'Very good, sir,' replied Evans and clambered back to his seat. Holmes swung into the carriage.

Quickly he explained the situation to Colonel Harden. 'There are enough of us to deal with them,' said the Colonel. 'I'm armed, so is the doctor.'

'No, no, Colonel,' said Holmes. 'I am sorry to prevent you from confronting your persecutors yet again, but we can make more valuable use of the situation.'

'How so?' growled Colonel Harden, with a distinct air of disappointment.

'First I must ask you to lend me your topcoat and hat, while you take mine.' He rummaged in his travelling bag and emerged with a fair wig. 'Sergeant Turley, if you will take Jay's coat and hat – he is almost your height and the wig will enhance the imposture. The rain gives us an excuse for muffling our faces.'

The changes were quickly made. 'Watson,' said Holmes, 'keep your eye to the rear window. It would be monstrously unlucky if they were to lose our track now.'

I swivelled and peered back through the rain. Well behind us I could just discern a hansom, making its way at no greater speed than our own.

I had perceived, in outline, what my friend intended to do. He was proposing that he and the Sergeant would disembark at the railway station in the guise of the Colonel and his son, hoping to lead our pursuers astray, and I felt uneasy.

'I don't like this, Holmes,' I said. 'The odds are two to one in our favour at present, but you are reducing them to three to two against. I don't like it.'

'Ah, Watson,' smiled Holmes, 'always the sportsman's eye, eh? Surely you take account of form and running, Watson? Drew's louts do not know what we are doing – we do. They will follow Sergeant Turley and me because they believe us to be the Colonel and Jay and because they have been told not to let us out of their sight. We shall give them such a run as they do not expect. In the meantime, you will take Colonel Harden home, leave Jay in safety, collect the Colonel's necessaries and make for Hereford from the nearest station. What could be simpler?'

'It could be deucedly dangerous for you and the Sergeant,' I complained.

'I will, if Colonel Harden can spare them, take a couple of his derringers. They will give us a little surprise advantage if things come to close quarters,' said Holmes, 'but I am sure they will be unnecessary.'

The Colonel handed over two of his small pistols and Holmes pocketed one and passed the other to Sergeant Turley.

'Take my Adams as well,' I suggested.

'Certainly not,' said Holmes. 'I have already reduced the Colonel's armament and you may have to protect him on your travels.'

We took the last corner before the station, still travelling slowly, and our driver's warning knocks came just as I spotted a face peering round the corner behind us. 'They see us,' I told Holmes.

'Excellent!' he exclaimed. 'Sergeant, be ready to jump out after me as soon as we stop.'

We slowed to a halt in the station yard and Holmes and the Sergeant swung out, their faces concealed in upturned collars. 'Wire me from Hereford!' called Holmes, and was gone into the rain.

Drew's carriage had increased its pace and was turning into the yard. Hastily I knocked on the roof-flap. As our driver opened it I shouted, 'Turn across the yard entrance! Block them if you can!'

He whipped up his horses instantly and swung the vehicle as tightly as he could, bringing it at an angle across the mouth of the station yard. Harden and I were flung about the interior as we strove to pull down the blinds.

The manœuvre succeeded. In a moment a torrent of curses met our ears as Drew's driver realised that he had no access to the station. Constable Evans let himself be thought the clumsiest cabman in London as he edged his horses back and forwards, without ever making way for the other vehicle.

A long whistle sounded from the station and, at last, Constable Evans slowly turned our conveyance out of the yard. Once around the corner he stopped and opened the flap.

'I had hoped to let the Sergeant and Mr Holmes away on the train,' he said, 'but two from that cab got out and ran for it when they heard the whistle. They might just have made it.'

'Never mind, Constable,' I said. 'You did very well to blockade them so long. Now let us carry on.'

As I sat back Colonel Harden passed me a cigar. 'Doctor,' he said, 'I had British officers under me in the war and I learned they were cool customers, but your friend beats all I have ever seen.'

It was a deserved compliment and I accepted it on Holmes' behalf, but as we rattled away southward into the rain I could not repress a feeling of foreboding, and my hand was never far from the butt of my Adams .450.

19

AMR'S GRAVE

Colonel Harden and I reached Hereford without incident and established ourselves in an hotel there. Immediately upon our arrival I wired our location to Baker Street, reply paid. No answer reached us that night.

The Colonel saw my concern for Holmes and did his best to distract me. On another occasion it would have been a considerable pleasure to hear his reminiscences of the war in which he had gained his reputation, a war which had loomed large in the press in my youth, but in the end he saw that my mind was wholly elsewhere.

'Come, doctor,' he said. 'By your own accounts Sherlock Holmes has wriggled out of far tighter spots and he will come up smiling again.' I acknowledged the truth of his remark, but nevertheless I retired to my room filled with a sense of foreboding.

At Winchester I had watched while Holmes had manœuvred Colonel Harden into volunteering himself as a stalking horse to draw out Drew's gang, but ever since that moment my friend's only thought had been to protect our client. Twice already he had put himself directly between Harden and his persecutors, at great risk on each occasion. It was a long time before I fell asleep.

With the morning there was still no response from Holmes, which I took as a sign that he had not returned to Baker Street. It did nothing to calm my fears but, whatever my friend's fate, I knew his intentions in Herefordshire and was determined to carry them out as far as I was able.

The Colonel and I agreed that the public library would be as good a starting point as any. There we were met by an amiable and willing assistant who was, nonetheless, unable to answer our queries.

'I cannot say that I know of such a grave in this country,' he said. 'There is Arthur's Stone at Dorstone, but that is said to be either the grave of Arthur or the stone from which he drew the sword.'

'Then can you tell us anything about the ancient kingdom of Ercing?' asked Colonel Harden.

'Ercing?' the assistant said. 'That rings a bell. Let me consult one of my colleagues a moment, gentlemen.'

He scurried away, to return a few minutes later with a sheaf of maps under his arm. He spread them across a table in a litter worthy of Holmes and showed us how the wide lands of Ercing had shrunk to a mere parish.

'So there you have it, gentlemen,' he said, as he ended his dissertation. 'If the grave you seek was in Ercing, then it is now in the Parish of Archenfield by Ross, or somewhere in that vicinity.'

We thanked him and returned to our hotel. No word had come from Holmes and, before leaving for Ross, I wired our destination.

We re-established ourselves at Ross and started our quest next morning at the public library, and here we were more successful. Although another assistant could not answer our questions, he referred us to a member of the public who was in the library. 'He is,' he said, 'a member of the Woolhope Club who are enthusiasts in local matters and he knows as much as any man alive about the legends of Herefordshire. He is a photographer and has photographed every place and monument of any consequence for many a mile around.'

'If he is a fellow photographer of antiquities,' said the Colonel, 'then it will be a pleasure to make his acquaintance.'

The introduction was effected and Harden and the stranger soon plunged deep into photographic details that were beyond me. I was uneasily aware that our enquiries might be leaving too broad a trail for Drew's men, and was content to let the Colonel pose as an American photographer with an interest in our antiquities, which, to be accurate, he was.

At length Colonel Harden shook his informant warmly by the hand and thanked him effusively for his help. As we left the building I could see that he was well pleased with his enquiry.

'I take it that we have better directions?' I said.

He laughed. 'Yes,' he said, 'but I fancy you will need to interpret them for me.'

He passed me the page of his pocket-book on which he had made notes of the stranger's information:

The TUMP at WORMLOW

'I don't know what that might mean to you,' he said, 'but our friend tells me that a tump is a hill or a mound in the local speech. He also says there is a spring in the vicinity.'

'Then we are looking for a mound at a place called Wormlow,' I said, 'wherever that may be.'

'It is a very few miles, according to our friend,' said Harden.

So it proved, and we were there by late morning. It revealed itself as a tiny village and the 'tump' lay close by, a grassy eminence surmounted by a few scrappy bushes that could hardly be described as trees. We walked around it, finding no distinguishing feature along its perimeter.

'It seems a humble sort of grave to shelter a son of Arthur,' remarked the Colonel, 'but we appear to have one of our markers and another may be nearby.'

'But if we have one grave and a well,' I mused, recalling the Glastonbury text, 'we must yet find another grave and three rings.'

'Our friend could not help us on those points,' said Harden, 'but if we have the right well, then there is a ring of some kind around it. Why don't we enquire?' he suggested, pointing with his stick at the village inn.

We took a simple but adequate meal at the inn, then questioned mine host. He knew of nothing in the immediate vicinity that might be another grave or anything that might be called a ring. The spring, he assured us, was only a short distance away, and he summoned one of his regulars to show us to it.

We paid our reckoning and walked out to our hired trap. Our guide, who had evidently taken not a little of the local cider, led our horse down a lane out of the village, perhaps not trusting himself to scramble aboard. At length we came to a gap in the irregular stone walls that framed the sunken lane, where we halted. Our guide pointed across the fields to a small pool.

'There 'tis, gentlemun,' he said, and sank immediately to rest in a squat at the roadside, still clutching the horse's rein. It was evident that we were not to be accompanied further. There were steps in the wall nearby and Harden and I clambered over and set out across the field.

Our arrival at the little pool led to a severe disappointment. Certainly it was fed by a spring, and a stream ran away from it, but nothing that could be interpreted as a ring seemed anywhere near; it stood among open fields.

'The instructions said to look from the gorse grave to the grave of Arthur's son,' recalled the Colonel, gazing back in the direction of the village, 'and whatever we are seeking is buried half-way to a ringed well. If we have Amr's grave and the right well, where the blazes are the rings and the other grave?'

We had stood and looked and seen nothing to our purpose. Now we started back to the road.

'Perhaps,' I said, 'the other grave is at some distance.'

'It cannot have been very far,' said Harden. 'Whoever laid out those directions meant them to lead to one spot only. To do so he had to be sure that his "half-way" could not be seriously inaccurate. I suspect he meant the kind of distance a man could easily pace out. If that's true, then we should see at least the ring, if not two other rings and a grave.'

His reasoning impressed but did not cheer me. 'I imagine,' I said, 'that many ancient constructions like Amr's grave must have vanished over the centuries.'

'Yes, indeed,' he said. 'Two hundred years ago your countrymen were using stones from Stonehenge and Avebury to build barns and blowing up the ruins at Glastonbury for building stone. What we are seeking may have vanished long ago.'

We were silent as we climbed back into the lane. Our assistant had fallen fast asleep, though still clutching our rein. While I went to waken him, Colonel Harden mounted the trap.

As I shook the still figure his battered billycock tumbled from his head and he pitched forward into the road. Impatient at his sottishness, I bent to shake him sharply when I perceived that the back of his head was dabbled with blood. My exploring fingers quickly revealed that the blood hid a considerable swelling, as though from a severe blow. I could not imagine how he had come by such an injury while seated alone at the lane's edge.

Hardly had I made this peculiar discovery than I heard a shout of alarm from the Colonel. I whirled about, to find him standing in the trap with raised whip. Around the conveyance stood three villainous individuals armed with cudgels.

I had barely grasped the situation when the attackers rushed at Harden. With a cracking blow of the whip he felled the leader, who reeled back on to his comrades. As I sprang round the horse to back him up, Harden took advantage of their disarray to leap down at my side.

He glanced around him then plucked at my sleeve and ran down the lane. I followed him as he vaulted over the low wall on the far side from the spring, and dashed across the field that presented itself, at a commendable speed for a man of his age. Even as we ran I mentally commended his line of retreat, for ahead of us I could see what appeared to be a small outcrop of woodland that might provide us with a refuge.

We were half-way towards it when our pursuers followed us over the wall and gave chase. I was about to call to Harden to draw his weapons and help me drive them off, when a pistol barked from behind us and a bullet sang past my ear.

20

A MEXICAN STAND-OFF

The belief that the Colonel and I had only to turn and draw our pistols vanished with that single shot, but it was followed by three more. Fortunately they were fired by men running hard across rough meadow and offered us no great threat, but they made clear the impossibility of defeating our attackers in the open.

We plunged into the edge of the wood and flung ourselves behind two trees. I was gasping for breath, but the Colonel recovered quickly and scanned the field. 'Six of them now,' he reported, 'and we don't know how many are armed.'

He pulled his two small pistols from his pockets. 'Two or three shots, please, doctor,' he requested.

'I doubt if I can do much harm from here,' I replied, for our pursuers had slowed to a walk and were still some distance away, 'nor will your derringers.'

'It'll tell them we are armed,' he said, 'and that will keep them at bay for the time being.'

He fired a few rounds and I joined in. It had the desired effect, inasmuch as Drew's party dropped into the rough grass for cover.

'Now we have a stronghold,' said the Colonel. 'The brush here is thick enough to hide our movements.'

'But we cannot now see them,' I said.

'It makes no odds,' he said. 'They won't rush us, for fear of us killing two or three, and they know we can't attack them because we're outnumbered and probably outgunned. Back home we call this kind of thing a "Mexican stand-off".'

Despite the gravity of our position the curious expression amused me. 'A Mexican stand-off?' I queried.

'I think you might call it an impasse,' he smiled, and I began to realise that the old warhorse was actually enjoying the situation.

'Can we not withdraw?' I asked.

'Where to? Behind us is more pasture, as long a run as we've just done, if not longer. They'd stand a good chance of taking us on the run.'

'Then we are trapped,' I said.

'Maybe not,' he replied. 'What time is sundown in these parts?'

Silently I cursed the fact that it was close to midsummer. 'About eight o'clock, I imagine. It should be fully dark by nine.'

He drew out his watch. 'Then we have about five hours,' he said. 'Let's inspect the fortifications.'

We circled the little wood, learning that it was about one hundred yards in diameter. At any point within it we were virtually invisible because of the thick underbrush, but it was surrounded by open meadow.

Harden cast a practised eye over the field at the rear. 'See there?' he asked. 'That hollow line in the grass?'

'Yes,' I said. 'It looks like the line of an old fence, or a field ditch.'

'It'll have to do,' he said. 'If nothing else happens by nightfall we'll crawl out along that in the dark. How many rounds do you have?'

'Three in hand and an unopened box in my pocket.'

'I have six or seven loaded and a fresh carton,' he said, 'so we're not short. We can afford a few rounds to keep them guessing where we are.'

Throughout the remainder of the day we moved separately about the perimeter of our fortress, snapping the odd shot out across the fields from different positions. Sometimes our shots brought return fire, all of it harmless. Gradually we concluded that the enemy had spaced themselves out in a wide circle round our refuge.

The summer day dragged on and it was as well that we were both old soldiers, used to the unique blend of danger and boredom which is a soldier's lot. Nonetheless, time hung heavy, and I brooded as much on Holmes' situation as on our own.

'I cannot understand,' I remarked at one point, 'why no one has come this way all afternoon.'

'I don't know where the road goes,' said the Colonel, 'but no one seems to travel on it. There are no stock in the fields round about, except a few sheep away over. They're fenced in so I guess there isn't even a boy with them.'

'But someone must have heard shots by now,' I argued.

'Don't your farmers shoot varmints?' Harden said. 'I reckon darkness is our best chance.'

'What if Drew's thugs have found the ditch or whatever it is?'

'They daren't stand up, so they can't see it,' said the Colonel. 'I suppose if we're really unlucky one of them might have crawled into it.'

The thought had not occurred to me. 'Suppose we blunder into them in the dark?' I asked.

'After dark guns will be dangerous to both sides, but we'll carry a full load with us when we go. They're spaced around us, so we shan't tangle with more than one. If we do, then at least we'll be pretty certain who he is and close enough to shoot him. After that we run like blazes, doctor.'

'Do you know,' I said, 'I believe you're enjoying this, Colonel!'

He smiled widely. 'Ever since I set foot in England this skunk Drew has dogged my footsteps, threatened my family, kidnapped my boy, tried to kill me and stolen my plates, and every time I got a chance to fight back, your Mr Holmes has pulled me out of the line. If we run into the whole boiling out there I'm going to settle some of the score.'

The sun reddened at last, and we were pleased to note that it was veiled by thin cloud. We hoped that the night might be a dark one. The Colonel took out a pocket-knife and cut two stout cudgels, while I continued patrolling and letting off an occasional shot until the last light was almost gone.

As darkness fell the fields turned to a uniform deep grey, unlit by moon or stars. We peered hard into the gloom, seeking any darker patch that might be one of our enemy, but saw none.

'Time to go,' hissed the Colonel. 'After you, doctor.'

Pistol in one hand and cudgel in the other I wriggled out from the undergrowth into the slight hollow in the field. Cautiously I crept a few yards, then waited for Harden. His soldierly skills had not rusted, for he slid down after me without a sound, and we began to crawl stealthily along the hollow.

We moved slowly, covering only a few yards at a time and then pausing, so as to avoid any noticeable disturbance of the grass. In this fashion we had covered nearly one third of the distance to the far wall of the field, and I was beginning to feel hopeful of our enterprise, when I ran my head against an obstruction in the darkness.

Drew's pickets must have been dozing at their task, for I had found one of them and he did not, initially, react. He had been lying in the narrow defile with his head towards us, and we were face to face. His slowness saved the situation for, as he gasped in surprise and attempted to move, I dealt him a stunning blow with the butt of my Adams.

My victim had time for only one startled cry before I felled him, but that sound rang out in the darkness. Immediately it was answered by calls from other positions in the darkened field.

Colonel Harden raised his head cautiously from the grass. 'They haven't located us,' he whispered. 'Let's go.'

We rolled the senseless thug out of our way and commenced crawling as fast as we dared towards our goal. Around us our pursuers were calling to each other with low cries.

'They'll work out who doesn't answer soon,' hissed Harden, 'and when they do they'll find us.'

In a crouching run we made towards the wall, while the shouts across the field seemed to indicate that our opponents had discovered the general direction of our escape. Nevertheless I believed we might reach our goal before they had located us precisely.

It was at this juncture that events took an unexpected turn against us. The thin clouds that had veiled the sky since late evening broke, allowing the moon's light to wash over the field.

'Down!' hissed Colonel Harden from behind me. 'Lie still!'

I dropped into the shelter of the hollow, my heart beating like a drum. Harden slowly raised his head. 'We're stymied,' he whispered. 'That confounded wall is lit up like a carnival. If we try for it they'll pick us off as we go over.'

We lay in silence, separately considering the situation. Suddenly the cries across the meadow changed. Now they seemed more like exclamations of alarm or surprise. I risked raising my head.

The velvet darkness had vanished and had been replaced by a clear pale light, in which every irregularity betrayed itself by a black shadow. As Colonel Harden had said, the wall of the field was a ribbon of white and to attempt to climb it would be madness. I scanned the field for Drew's men, spotting here and there what may have been heads among the grass.

Then I saw the cause of their alarm. Pouring across the lower end of the field and swirling towards us was a curious white mass. Now I saw one of our pursuers rise from his hide-out and run for the copse, heedless of exposure. I plucked Harden's sleeve and summoned him to look. He gazed intently for several seconds. Suddenly a new sound reached us, faint but unmistakable among the oaths of Drew's gang.

'Sheep!' we both exclaimed. Somehow the flock from the adjacent field had found its way through the wall and was exploring our meadow.

'That's all the diversion we needed,' said the Colonel. 'Run for it, doctor!'

We abandoned concealment and sprinted towards the field's boundary, and reached it without pursuit. As we scrambled over it a couple of ill-aimed shots went off behind us. In a moment we had dropped into the inky darkness on the far side and squatted to take our bearings.

We had come into a narrow cart-track between two fields and we started along it in the direction of the village. We had not gone far when a blacker shape loomed out of the dark track ahead of us. To our astonishment it proved to be our own hired horse and trap.

'What the blazes is that doing here?' demanded Harden, and we approached it cautiously.

A droning sound reached us and as we drew close we could see a muffled figure huddled in the driver's seat. The reek of cheap cider was about the man and he was snoring rhythmically. Harden gazed back the way we had come.

'Let's have a light,' he said. 'They are not following us.'

I risked striking a match and lifted it to illuminate the trap's occupant. Our surprise was compounded when we saw that it was our guide of the afternoon. Now he huddled in a cape of sacking, his old jacket tied with farmer's twine and his battered billycock slung low over his face. His stentorian snores fluttered his tobacco-stained whiskers.

'Lord!' exclaimed the Colonel, as I reached up to shake the old drunkard awake. 'He must be very anxious to earn a shilling!'

'Come now, Colonel,' said the voice of Holmes. 'You assured me at Winchester that expense was no object!'

Laughing heartily we clambered aboard, as Holmes flung off his cape of sackcloth, whipped up the horse and made away for the village.

STRATAGEMS AND RESCUES

Holmes had commandeered the inn's spartan accommodation and, after a welcome supper, I was soon asleep in a little room under the eaves. It was not until we had reassembled over breakfast that we were able to persuade him to tell us how he and Sergeant Turley had escaped from Drew's men and how he had come to our assistance on the previous night.

'You will recall,' he said, 'that as the Sergeant and I entered the railway station, there was a train about to depart?'

We nodded and he went on, 'We had believed that was our good fortune. It mattered not where that train was bound if we could leave the station before our pursuers caught up with us.'

An indicator board showed that the train was bound for the south coast and Holmes and the Sergeant had sprung aboard. They were congratulating themselves on the fact that the train had no corridor, when they saw Drew's henchmen sprinting down the platform. At that very moment the train began to draw out of the station. Unluckily, the pursuers had seen which compartment held Holmes and his ally and, before the train had gathered its full speed, they succeeded in scrambling into it.

Their surprise must be imagined when they found that the compartment was completely empty. Breathless and dispirited they slumped into seats and discussed whether they had inadvertently entered the wrong compartment.

The train was now travelling at full speed and, with a shriek of its whistle and a sudden blast of air through the compartment's open window, it plunged into a tunnel. Darkness descended on them and thick smoke from the engine rolled into the compartment.

One of them rose, coughing, and stepped across the carriage to pull up the window. As he fumbled in the smoky darkness for the window's securing strap, a steely hand grasped him and flung him down on to a seat. The unmistakable cold ring of a pistol's mouth was pressed firmly against his temple and a stern voice commanded, 'Do not move!'

In a trice, and before he or his astonished confederate could react, the train had left the tunnel. The smoke was sucked out of the open window and the tall figure of Holmes materialised, pressing one of the Colonel's pistols against the head of one man while the other covered his colleague. Behind him the compartment's open door swung with the movement of the train.

'If either of you moves an inch,' said Holmes, 'I shall not hesitate to shoot.'

The two villains remained pale-faced and motionless. 'That is very sensible of you,' said Holmes and raised his voice. 'Sergeant Turley,' he called, 'you may join us now.'

The wind-swept police officer slid through the door from his hiding-place on the train's footboard and pulled it shut behind him. Holmes passed him a pistol. 'Now,' he told their prisoners pleasantly, 'you will sit on either side at that end of the compartment and Sergeant Turley and I will sit at this end and look for any opportunity to shoot you.'

The captives took up their position and sat for a little while, staring at their captors like frightened rabbits. Then one of them began to speak.

'We didn't mean any harm,' he said. 'We was merely told off to follow the Colonel and his boy.'

'I know what were your purposes,' said Holmes, 'and those of your master. If you are lucky enough to return to him, be so good as to inform him that the object of his search is known to me and that I will spare no effort to see that he fails.'

He drew his watch from his pocket and glanced out of the window. 'I think,' he said to Turley, 'that we shall soon be at our destination.'

'Our destination, sir?' queried the Sergeant.

'We must travel to the coast in order to catch a train back to London,' said Holmes, 'but I have no intention of sharing the journey with these two. Besides, I imagine that they have boarded the train without tickets.'

'What are you going to do, Mr Holmes?' asked one of the prisoners, fearfully.

'Do?' said Holmes. 'If all goes well I am going to do nothing. You, on the other hand, are going to open the door beside you.'

Their eyes started. 'You ain't going to push us out!' exclaimed one.

'Certainly not!' said my friend, 'You are going to step out of the train as we pass through the next curve,' and he made a threatening motion with his pistol. 'Up!' he commanded.

They rose like automata and began to open the door. As soon as it was free the motion of the train swung it wide open. The train was passing through a chalk cutting in the downs and a wall of limestone was visible beyond the open door.

'If you are not brisk about it,' said Holmes, 'the train will speed up,' and he motioned with the pistol again.

At the very brink they balked. Holmes fired one shot, and as it whistled past their heads, the two miscreants leapt shrieking out of the train.

Holmes pulled the door to and resumed his seat, putting away his pistol and taking his pipe from his pocket. 'I dare say that I shouldn't have permitted you to do that,' remarked Sergeant Turley.

'I have merely saved the South-Western Railway the trouble of catching a pair of rogues macing the rattler,' said Holmes, and the Sergeant laughed.

When Holmes had recited this narrative both Harden and I were chuckling. 'But how did you land up here so providentially?' asked the Colonel.

'Providence had nothing to do with it,' replied Holmes. 'By the time the good Sergeant and I reached the terminus it was too late to return to London and we were forced to wait until the morning. During that night I gave some little extra thought to the meaning of the Glastonbury fragment, so that when I arrived in London I felt obliged to make certain arrangements. When I had done so I returned to Baker Street and saw your telegrams.'

He poured himself another coffee and drew a slip of paper from his pocket. 'I had telegraphed to your Ross address, asking you to confirm a fresh rendezvous, but so far from any reply from you I received this from Porlock.'

He passed us the paper, which said only:

D has sent men to Hereford.

'I dared not underestimate Drew's intelligence and I felt sure that he would readily pick up your trail,' he said. 'I feared that you might run into difficulty. A wire to Ross revealed that you had gone to Wormlow, and thither I followed post-haste.'

'But your disguise – the trap in the lane?' I queried. 'How on earth did you know that Colonel Harden and I were trapped in that field?'

'I was pursuing my enquiries at this very hostelry,' said Holmes, 'when I was interrupted by the arrival of one Tacky Boatman. It was he who revealed your plight to me.'

'Tacky Boatman?' I exclaimed. 'Who may he be?'

'Mr Boatman,' said my friend, 'was engaged by you to show you a spring, in the course of which harmless duty he was cudgelled by Drew's louts. A small expenditure on cider soothed his hurts and secured his collaboration and the loan of his distinctive costume. Disguised as him I surveyed the land and became aware that somebody armed

141

with derringers and an Adams was occupying the copse. It was an easy inference that your only way out would be by the ditch after dark. I merely borrowed a flock of sheep to assist you.'

He finished his narrative with the air of a conjurer explaining a very basic trick. Once again Harden and I were moved to chuckle.

'It seems I fall deeper into your debt every day,' said Harden.

'Think nothing of it, Colonel,' said Holmes. 'Watson will tell you that I strive to avoid those problems which are usually the province of private enquiry agents and seek for those which exhibit distinctive features. I am your debtor for bringing to me a case which has so many singular features about it.'

Holmes' recital of his adventures had driven from my recollection the failure of our survey of Wormlow. Now it returned and I felt obliged to mention it immediately.

'Holmes,' I said, 'you have evidently followed the line of reasoning which brought us here, but I should tell you that both the Colonel and I believe we are on a false trail. The mound nearby may well be the grave of Arthur's son, and certainly we found the spring, but there is no other grave nor any ring that we could see.'

The Colonel nodded in agreement, but to my surprise Holmes merely smiled slightly.

'I believe I mentioned,' he said, 'that I had given further consideration to the Glastonbury pattern. My second examination of the problem revealed that I had fallen into an easy trap.'

'How come?' asked Harden.

'I have always believed that the obvious answer is usually the correct one,' said Holmes, 'but that, in itself, may be a trap. Too swift an acceptance of the obvious may leave a less likely alternative unrevealed. That, I fear, is what I permitted myself to do with the Glastonbury message.'

We stared at him, nonplussed.

'On my return to London,' he continued, 'I was able, not only to confirm my error, but to arrive at a more logical solution of our problem and to make arrangements accordingly.'

'To make arrangements?' I queried.

'Yes, indeed,' he responded. 'Among other things I have acquired for us accommodation in the vicinity of Haverfordwest.'

'Haverfordwest!' I exclaimed. 'But that is far from here – in western Wales!'

'So I believe,' he replied, unperturbed, 'but that is where we must go once we have collected your luggage from Ross.'

SHERLOCK HOLMES' MISTAKE

We arrived in Haverfordwest in the early evening, where a driver with a sturdy country equipage met us. As the day darkened we rolled through the countryside north of the town, into the so-called Prescelly Mountains.

They are not properly mountains, but a range of hills that lie almost due east and west in Pembrokeshire, their westerly extremity close to the coast. Whatever they may lack in height they repay amply in atmosphere, for the mood of their landscape changes at every turn of the dusty country lanes and every slightest variation of the weather.

Although it was nearly midsummer when we came among them, it had been a breezy day, and ragged clouds were moving fast across the evening sky. At one moment we would be jogging through a cheerful valley, the green hillsides dabbled with gorse blossoms bright in the evening sun, then a skein of cloud would darken the scene and we would be in a narrow grey-green defile where the hills pressed close on the winding road and heaps of weirdly shaped boulders straggled down the slopes as though to block our path. Here and there along our way I spotted stones that had evidently been set in position, if not shaped, by the hand of man, and these ancient sentinels were most of the evidence of occupation that we saw, for houses and farms were few and far between.

Holmes sat with hands folded on the handle of a country ash, silently absorbing the passing scene. Colonel Harden looked from side to side with every turn of our conveyance.

'By heavens, Mr Holmes,' he exclaimed at one point, 'if I had known what lay among these hills I would not have wasted so much time in London and at Stonehenge. This landscape is wonderfully primitive.'

'You must not berate yourself for echoing the mistake of our own historians,' said Holmes. 'They too have addressed their devotions to Stonehenge and Avebury without considering what lies in these hills, yet the profusion of ancient burials and Stone Age circles hereabouts suggests that this was a place of great importance to our forefathers.'

'But hardly anyone lives here now,' I protested, 'and I cannot recall a single reference in the history books.'

'With the possible exception of political essays,' said Holmes, 'there is probably no more misleading a class of literature than history books. Your own fictitious versions of my cases are paragons of accuracy beside the ordinary school history text.'

'I see you hold historians in very low esteem,' I joked.

'I hold them in no esteem whatsoever,' he replied, ignoring my attempt at pleasantry. 'They rarely observe at first hand, they feed upon each other's mistakes, and they vie with each other to construct the most preposterous interpretation of what they believe to be the facts.'

'Then I must take my camera to some of these old stones,' said Harden, 'and see if the eye of science can reveal a few genuine facts for the historians to chew over.'

'You shall have your opportunity,' said Holmes, 'for we shall adopt the guise of archaeologists while we pursue our researches in Wales.'

We had crossed over the ridge of the hills and dropped down on the northerly side. Now we wound into a small valley, from which the sun had already retreated, but a lamp glowed in a window beside the lane ahead of us. We pulled up outside the lighted window, in front of a low stone cottage, and, as we climbed stiffly down from the vehicle, our driver carried our luggage inside.

'There you are, then,' he said, when he had done. 'Mrs Williams has laid you supper, as you asked, sir, and I hope all is to your liking.'

Holmes thanked the man and paid him and he trudged away into the gathering darkness while we took possession of our new lodgings.

The interior of the cottage was larger than I had anticipated, the entire front consisting of one large room. At one end of this room two high-backed wooden settles flanked a fire-place, while at the rear, between two doors, stood a plain table laden with our refreshments.

When we had removed the dust of the railway and the road we made short work of the excellent cold provisions and, somewhat relieved of the gloom engendered by the landscape, I lit my pipe and thought to question Holmes.

'Well, Holmes,' I said, 'you have brought us at short notice almost all the way across Wales, without a word of explanation. May we now know your reasons?'

'Watson,' he said, reprovingly, 'you know very well that I have always maintained that results are more impressive than methods. I have already told you that I found myself in error.'

'It can only have been a small error, or the text would not have made sense,' observed Harden.

'But that,' said Holmes, 'was precisely the problem, as your researches at Wormlow proved.'

'Surely,' I said, 'the fact that Wormlow proved not to be the place does not, of itself, establish that the directions are wrong?'

'Well argued, Watson,' said Holmes. 'I see that you have derived a little benefit from my frequent homilies on the nature of deductive inference, and in absolute terms you are right. However, if you cast your mind back to the reason why we selected Wormlow, you will see my meaning.'

'We went there because we believed that the grave of Arthur's son was there,' said Harden, 'and, so far as we know, we found it. We also found a well. It was the other markers that were absent.'

'Exactly,' said Holmes. 'We began by seeking the grave of Arthur's son and, having found it, realised it was the wrong place. Had I not realised that there was an error in my approach, that would have proved it. If our translation of the pattern was correct, and the inferences we drew from it, then Wormlow would have been the place. It was not, and thereby we have proved my belief that I was wrong.'

'In what way?' I asked.

'Let us reconsider the directions,' he said, and taking out his pocket-book he wrote them on a page. 'There,' he said, 'apart from the biblical reference, is the text as we discovered it.'

We looked at the page and agreed:

```
–   –   –   –   –   –   –   –   –   O   M   –
–   N   G   I   N   G   S   T   O   N   E   P
–   –   S   E   Y   E   G   R   E   A   T   E
–   A   S   T   E   T   O   T   H   –   –   E
–   –   N   G   E   S   *   A   T   T   E   G
O   R   S   E   G   R   A   V   E   L   O   K
E   T   O   Y   E   G   R   A   V   E   O   F
–   –   –   –   U   R   S   S   O   N   N   E
*   H   A   L   F   W   A   Y   E   T   –   –
Y   E   R   I   N   –   –   D   W   E   L   L
–   I   T   T   L   Y   E   S   T   O   –   –
R   M   E   S   S   P   A   N   N   E   D   E
E   P   –   *   C   U   R   S   E   D   –   E
```

'I recall', he went on, 'expatiating on the importance in any analysis of the recognition of patterns, but I confess I overlooked the existence of one here,' and he tapped the paper.

'I have to admit that I do not see it,' said Harden.

'Consider the points of reference, as they are given,' said Holmes, and recited them. 'Hanging stone – ye great waste – three ringes – gorse grave – ye grave of Arthur's son – ye ringed well. Is there not something peculiar in the references?'

147

'I still do not see it,' I said.

'There are six points,' said Holmes, 'yet three have the definite article "ye" and three do not.'

Harden and I were totally bewildered.

'Does that not suggest that there is some difference between "hanging stone", "three ringes", and "gorse grave" and the other points?'

'Well, yes,' said Harden, slowly, 'but what of it?'

' "Ye hanging stone",' said Holmes, 'would indicate a particular, known, stone, from which one might start with confidence. Remove the definite article and it becomes any hanging stone. Even if the instructions indicated the area that would be insufficiently precise.'

'Then there is a missing part that defines the area?' I suggested.

'But there was not,' said Holmes, 'for the message commenced with the biblical text that defined the subject, and ended with what was undoubtedly a curse upon any who disturbed the hidden thing.'

'Then I don't know what we can do,' remarked Harden.

'We can consider,' said Holmes, 'whether we were wrong in adopting the reading "hanging stone".'

'There are few alternatives,' I said. 'Ranging stone, ringing stone, singing stone, winging stone – none of them seems to make as much sense as hanging stone.'

'Not in English, I grant you,' said Holmes, 'but I had wondered before why a monk who was most probably a Celt of some variety, and whose working language was Latin, wrote his instructions in English.'

'But they are in English, nevertheless,' protested Harden.

'The words,' said Holmes, 'are in English, but their meaning is in another language.'

While I pondered on this strange remark a thoughtful expression passed over the Colonel's face. After a moment he said, 'I don't know about England, but there are ringing stones in America. I've seen them.'

'Really?' I said. 'What are they?'

'There are rocks on the Delaware River, in Bucks County, Pennsylvania, that ring like bells. A few years ago I was visiting up there and I passed an evening at a meeting of a historical society. There was a doctor there who played melodies on some chunks of rock. They are some kind of volcanic deposit.'

Holmes smiled. 'I think you are on the wrong track, Colonel. I suggest that you remember that we are not in the States and that we are not, indeed, in England. Now, if you will excuse me, I shall turn in. There are preparations which I must make tomorrow.'

SHERLOCK HOLMES WATCHES

A fresh, sunny morning woke me as Mrs Williams, a short, sturdy Welshwoman, brought me hot water. While I shaved I heard her bustling about in the kitchen and I entered the cottage's wide front parlour to find Colonel Harden already seated at the table. The windows were open, showing a view of sunlit hills that banished my forebodings of the previous night, and an appetising aroma drifted through from the kitchen.

I sat down and the Colonel poured me a cup of coffee. 'Good morning, doctor,' he said. 'Mr Holmes is up and away early.'

I was startled, for I had imagined that Holmes was still in his bed. 'Up and away!' I exclaimed. 'It is most unlike him.'

'Then I guess he must have some purpose,' said the Colonel, 'and I imagine that he'll explain his purpose or not, just as he pleases.'

Mrs Williams had just served Harden and me when the latch of the front door clicked and Holmes strode in. His ash stick was in his hand, his hair blown by the breeze and his colour high. He rubbed his hands and advanced smiling on the table.

'A very good morning, gentlemen,' he said warmly. 'Watson, I believe your recommendations to exercise may have some worth. A brisk walk across the moors this morning has considerably sharpened my appetite.'

In my long experience of Sherlock Holmes he almost never indulged in exercise for its own sake, despite my constant urgings, nor did he readily break the peculiar patterns of his behaviour. Now I knew that his heightened colour and his smile derived not so much from the morning breezes, but from the working out of some prediction he had made to himself. I knew, also, that it would be pointless to question him until he was ready to reveal his knowledge.

When we had broken our fast Holmes lit his pipe and smiled upon us again. 'I have asked Mrs Williams to make us up a cold luncheon,' he said. 'If you will bring your camera, Colonel, we can support our character as archaeologists as well as enjoying this fine day.'

'I had understood that you had preparations to make,' I said, surprised at my friend's holiday mood.

'The first half of my preparations are complete,' he said, 'and the second half must wait upon others and may take a day or so. We may as well take advantage of the interval.'

Harden fetched his apparatus and we set out in Mr Williams' sturdy little cart. Holmes took us to the western end of the hills, where they climbed up from a gently sloping moor to a gaunt and ragged pinnacle of rock, like a natural castle crowning the ridge. From its heights we looked down on the shores of the Principality and out across a sparkling sea to a distant smudge which Holmes declared to be the Irish shore.

On the moor itself Holmes showed us the tumbled rings of stone that marked the dwellings of our ancestors and the Colonel plied his camera on them. All the time Holmes kept up a running stream of information about these ancient monuments and the Celto-Iberians who had built them. He explained how his studies in the Chaldean tongue, which he believed to be the mother of all European languages, had led him to learn the history of our forefathers and whence they came. He peopled the silent moors for us with little, swarthy, dark-eyed men who had come, according to their own legends, from a land 'beyond Constantinople' and had brought with them a tongue descended from the great mother language and a worship descended from the eastern cult of the Great Mother.

Gazing at a single stone standing on an empty, heather-clad moor, he told us how the people who erected it and the purpose it served both had their origins in the great temples of North Africa and the Mediterranean. He was always fascinating when in this mode, and I could listen to him with interest for hours at a time, but on that day I was aware that his mind was not entirely in the far past. I knew him well enough to perceive that, when he swung his stick around the horizon, he was scanning the landscape with his extraordinary eyes.

We came in the afternoon to a path along a northern slope of the hills. As we turned around the shoulder of the hill there opened before us as spectacular a view as any I have met with in three continents.

Out of the flower-spattered grass in front of us rose ragged pillars of grey rock, which supported a flat roof of the same. It was evidently one of those burial monuments that are to be found all over our western counties, and must have been the resting-place of someone who had deserved the respect of his people, for they cannot have been unaware of the dramatic beauty of the spot. Beneath us the hill sloped sharply to where an inlet of the sea lay sparkling, and beyond it further hills marched north-wards.

While Harden took pictures, Holmes and I unshipped and laid out Mrs Williams' provisions. The sun was high in a cloudless sky and we ate in the shade of the ancient tomb. Our scramblings about the hills, together with an ample lunch, soon made me drowsy and in a short while I was asleep, propped comfortably against one of the stone pillars.

The sun had slipped quite a way down the sky when I awoke and found that Harden too had succumbed to sleep. Holmes was nowhere to be seen, but the Colonel woke as I clambered to my feet.

'Where is Holmes?' I asked him.

'He said he would walk off his meal,' said Harden, 'and he set out in that direction.' He pointed south.

I strolled up to the ridge behind us and looked around me. At length I discerned Holmes, a couple of hundred yards away, standing in the shade of a tree with a pair of field-glasses to his eyes. His position spoke of conceal-ment and, even at a distance, I could see that his use of the glasses was not casual.

I slipped quietly back to the monument, deep in thought. It was evident that, despite his attempts to distract the Col-onel and me, Holmes feared we were being observed. I reflected on the ambush at Wormlow and considered that we were now in even more remote and less populated country; an attack by Drew's men in these hills might well leave us without cover or support. I resolved to be on my guard at all times, but not to mention the matter to our client.

Holmes rejoined us a few minutes later, passing off his absence as another constitutional, and, after finishing the remains of our provisions, we set out for the cottage.

We passed the evening around the table in the parlour, discussing the sights we had seen during the day, and Holmes was again an erudite and witty commentator on them, yet still he was on guard; still I sensed a watchful, listening Holmes that was not entirely concealed by the informative companion.

We lit the lamp as sunset reddened the hills beyond the windows; darkness fell, owls hooted in the gloom and we remained around the table, smoking and chatting, but I did not believe that Holmes' mind was fully on our con-versation for one moment. My own senses were stretched by the knowledge of my friend's suspicions and I had dif-ficulty in concealing from my companions my alarm at the slightest disturbance. Soon I realised that Harden was equally distracted.

A night-bird called close to our open window and the Colonel started. 'What was that?' he asked.

'The local fauna celebrating the darkness,' said Holmes easily, and continued his remarks.

The same call came again, and Harden rose from the table. 'I don't know your birds,' he said grimly, 'but that one sounds pretty human to me. I think I'll just take a look around.'

Holmes rose as well. 'Forgive me, Colonel, but the protection of my client is paramount. If there is scouting to be done, then I really believe that the duty is mine.'

With a swift movement he doused the lamp and, by the time our eyes had grown accustomed to the gloom, he had slipped out of the door.

We waited in the darkened room, both of us peering cautiously from the windows, but the shadowed landscape revealed nothing.

'What is it that Mr Holmes expects?' asked Harden.

'Expects?' I queried.

'Doctor, your friend has been on tenterhooks all day. He expects something to happen. Has he revealed it to you?'

'Colonel,' I said, 'you have seen sufficient of Sherlock Holmes to know that he does not readily reveal his deductions and expectations to anybody until they are complete. I have learned to be patient and to repose my confidence in his absolute loyalty to his client, his indomitable courage and his singular mental processes.'

At that moment the latch clicked and Holmes stepped back into the room. Relighting the lamp, he smiled at us.

'If you had believed,' he said, 'that we are surrounded by Drew's minions, I can set your minds at rest. There is nothing more threatening than a few sheep out on the moors and we can rest in peace. Tomorrow, I believe, I can bring this affair to a conclusion for you, Colonel.'

With no further explanation he bade us good-night.

On the next morning he was, again, before us in rising, but so far from taking an early morning stroll he greeted us at the breakfast table. Mrs Hudson had forwarded the London papers and, in a very little time, he had turned our Welsh retreat into an imitation of Baker Street, with a litter of newspapers about his feet as he browsed through them.

The Colonel and I finished our breakfast and Harden became visibly impatient as my friend continued to sit over his coffee and lit another cigarette.

'Mr Holmes,' said the Colonel, at length, 'I had understood you to say that the affair would end today. Is there something we should be doing?'

'I do not believe so,' said Holmes, and reapplied himself to the newspapers.

Mrs Williams emerged from the kitchen and, after assuring Holmes that she had made his arrangements, left for her home. When she was gone, Holmes folded the last paper and dropped it among its fellows on the floor. He drew his revolver from his pocket and spun the cylinder.

'Now,' he said, 'if you will both be good enough to check your weapons, I shall show you a few more of the antiquities of this singular region, after which I think we shall be able to locate the Devil's Grail. Shall we go, gentlemen?'

24

THE SERPENT'S TEMPLE

We drove beneath a bright late morning sun along the valley, until we reached the easterly limit of the hills. Holmes halted our equipage below a bald rounded eminence and, taking a hurricane lantern from the cart and his ash stick in his other hand, strode away up the slope without a word.

We followed him upwards until he reached the summit and paused beside a cairn of grey stones, partly covered with coarse grass. Nearby a rough track scored the ground and stretched westward along the ridge. Holmes pointed with his stick as we joined him by the cairn.

'The locals call that the Robbers' Road,' he said, 'for it carried Irish invaders into the heart of Wales in olden times.'

'And the pile of stones?' queried the Colonel.

'That is said to be a grave,' said Holmes. 'It is called Bedd Arthur – the Grave of Arthur.'

'But surely', I said, 'we saw the site of Arthur's burial at Glastonbury?'

'Certainly,' said Holmes. 'Pray be so kind as to lend me a match, Watson.'

I passed him a box and he set about lighting the lantern that he carried. When it was burning steadily he turned the wick low and set the lamp firmly on top of the mound of stones. Before we could ask him his purpose he was striding back down the hill.

For the remainder of the day we travelled, apparently at Holmes' whim, backwards and forwards, across and around the line of hills, pausing here and there while he pointed out another antiquity to Colonel Harden. Many were simply single stones or pairs of stones, thrusting up like gaunt, grey fingers from the moss and coarse grass of the hillsides, but once we halted on a dreary stretch of moorland, where a complete ring of some fifteen small stones stood, not one being more than three feet high. A few yards away two larger stones stood separately, with little pools in the moss about them.

'What is this place called?' asked the Colonel.

'In the Welsh, Gors Fawr,' said Holmes.

The American thought had. 'Fawr I know,' he said. 'It means big or great, but this is the smallest ring I've ever seen.'

He busied himself taking photographs, for the sun was now lowering fast, while Holmes and I spread out our provisions. Once the Colonel had finished we sat and watched the shadows grow, as the sun sank in a sulphur-yellow sky behind the hills.

A covering of cloud had followed the sun down the sky, so that the twilight was swift and darker than usual. Now, as we repacked the cart and set out again, the hills showed that eerie aspect that they had revealed on our first arrival. Holmes, however, seemed unaffected by the gloom, and both Harden and I remarked that his watchfulness had disappeared.

It was almost completely dark when Holmes halted our equipage again. We had come to a lonely stretch of road which ran by a jumble of boulders among the wayside undergrowth. Holmes jumped down and detached one of the lamps. Harden and I followed and stood, peering into the gloom to find a reason for our visit. Holmes lifted the lamp high and, with its aid, the clumps of stone began to resolve themselves into groups. At last we could make out that we stood beside two stone rings, similar to the one at Gors Fawr.

'More rings yet!' exclaimed Harden. 'But it is too dark for photography, Mr Holmes.'

Holmes smiled. 'I have not brought you here to take pictures,' he said. 'I promised you that we should solve a mystery today. Look yonder,' and he pointed beyond the two circles and hefted his lantern higher.

'Three rings!' exclaimed Harden and I together, as the light revealed another ring.

Holmes laughed. 'Not quite,' he said, 'for the third circle has been partially destroyed, but there were once three and I'll vow there were three when the object that we seek was hidden.'

Harden had wandered away and was now inside the circle to our left. At the limit of the lantern's light he stooped and called back to us. 'A grave! There is a grave here!'

I turned to Holmes. 'Could it be . . .?' I began.

'Certainly,' said my friend. 'It is the Gorse Grave in the directions.'

'Can you be sure?' asked Harden as he rejoined us.

'It is beyond doubt,' replied Holmes, 'for the Welsh name of this spot is Eithbed – the Gorse Grave.'

He swung around, lifting the light again. 'Look!' he commanded, and pointed to the right-hand circle, where the lantern's beam flashed yellow on a patch of water at its heart.

Harden and I stood, looking from the dark mound at the centre of one ring to the reflection glowing in the other. 'Three rings,' said the Colonel, slowly, 'the Gorse Grave and a ringed well. We need only the grave of Arthur's son to give us our sight line.'

Holmes had pulled his field-glasses from his coat pocket. Now he focused them into the darkness. After a minute he passed the glasses to Harden.

'Look there!' he instructed, and pointed across the hills. Harden levelled the glasses and looked, then passed them to me. As my eyes focused I could see a spot of yellow light twinkling on the ridge.

'Your lantern!' I exclaimed. 'That is the marker?'

'Exactly,' said Holmes, and took the glasses from me. Walking to the centre of the left-hand ring, he stood on the hummock of the Gorse Grave. 'Colonel Harden,' he said, 'you are the taller. Will you be kind enough to stand between me and that distant light?'

The Colonel moved into position and Holmes asked him to raise his hand. Now my friend commanded the American to move left or right until he was satisfied that Harden was exactly in front of the distant lantern.

'Watson,' called Holmes, 'kindly mark the Colonel's position by placing a stone in front of his feet.'

I hurried to do so and Holmes lowered the glasses. 'Now,' he said, 'it should be a simple matter to locate our quarry.' Stepping to our little cart he took from it a pick-axe and shovel.

As he paced out the distance between the rings, I took off my coat in preparation for the exhumation. Holmes located his spot and turned to me.

'Fetch the tools, Watson,' he said, and began peeling off his own coat. Harden raised the lantern and we set to at the spot which Holmes had indicated.

It might be thought that the simple physical exercise of swinging the pickaxe would have driven vagrant thoughts from my mind, but our funereal activities brought eerie imaginings. The thump and rattle of our pick and shovel rang and echoed across the hillside and I could not but be aware of the ancient stones about us. As our lantern moved, its light caught the gnarled stones and the twisted clumps of brush that clothed the slope. I became aware that beyond the left-hand circle stretched a row of dark shapes that were stone burial chambers. More than once, as the circle of lamplight moved, I could have sworn that I saw dark figures moving among the ancient sepulchres, but I dashed the perspiration from my brow and applied myself to the task at hand.

The night was warm and the ground in which we dug solid. If anyone had disturbed this spot it had not been for a great many years. The task we had set ourselves was not easy, but gradually we began to form a decent-sized pit, in which Holmes and I stood and wielded our tools. After a while Holmes borrowed the lamp from the Colonel and turned it within the confines of the hole we had dug.

'See', he said, 'where the surface has been broken before and the soil beneath disturbed? If Drew's quest does not end here it will only be because we have been forestalled. This is definitely a spot where something has been buried.'

We slogged on, streaming with perspiration in the warm night, exchanging no words, our labours punctuated only by the blows of the pickaxe and spade. Despite Holmes' assurances, I was always aware of the dark hummock that lay at the heart of the nearby circle, of the stone tombs crouching on the dark slope and of the distant point of light on the hilltop that marked yet another grave. I could not prevent myself from wondering what savage rites had been practised here and what evidence we might, at the spade's next turn, reveal.

Nevertheless our efforts bore fruit, to the extent that the pit around Holmes and me deepened until we stood chest-deep. Holmes paused in his digging and measured the depth with his eye.

'It lies two arms' span deep,' he quoted. 'If it is here we must be standing on it.'

Scarcely had he spoken the words than my pickaxe drove into something more solid than earth, something that emitted a solid sound of impact.

Holmes ordered me out of the pit and took the lantern again. Carefully he scanned the excavation's floor and then began to pry at certain points with the pick's point. Harden and I knelt at the hole's edge, tense with the age-old thrill of the treasure- seeker. Among the moving shadows in the pit we could see that Holmes was outlining and freeing from the soil a large, dark object some three feet long and perhaps two across.

At last Holmes straightened. 'Be so kind as to fetch me a rope, Watson. I think we have succeeded.'

Quickly I brought a rope from the cart and in a very short while Holmes had the object securely tied. He scrambled from the pit with our help and, together, we manœuvred the dark bundle out of the earth in which it had lain so long.

The lantern's light showed us that our trophy was coated heavily with some kind of pitch, underneath which there seemed to be a wrapping of stout hide, heavily and tightly stitched. Holmes took his stick and heaved the parcel over, so that we could see that it was undamaged apart from a ragged hole where it had been struck by my pickaxe. Inside it had been packed with sand.

In part I was as eager as a child at Christmas to see the bundle opened, but at the same time I had the feeling that we had dragged something ancient from its hiding-place in this pagan temple of death and that, when we saw the object of our efforts, we might wish to have left it in its secret tomb.

I had no chance to resolve my conflicting emotions, for, as the three of us stood recovering our breath, a voice spoke quietly in the darkness.

'Step away from the bundle, gentlemen. There are three pistols levelled at you.'

It was the unmistakably distorted voice of Drew.

25

FIRE AND BRIMSTONE

The night breeze was warm but the sound of that voice chilled me to the core. Nevertheless, I could not help observing that Sherlock Holmes seemed remarkably unsurprised by the interruption.

Holmes, Harden and I drew back from the bundle lying at the pit's edge and three figures materialised out of the gloom beyond the lantern light, each carrying a pistol. The central one was Drew. On his left was a slight, pale-faced man and to his right a red-faced individual whose downcast eyes seemed always to dart from side to side.

'Will you not introduce us to your colleagues?' asked Holmes. 'Then allow me. Gentlemen, we are at the mercy of ex-Detective Sergeant Drew, formerly of Scotland Yard. To his left is his former colleague Sergeant Malcolm and on his right, their erstwhile solicitor, Mr Clive, whose efforts on their behalf were so successful that all three have spent some years in Her Majesty's prisons.'

'Scoff while you can, Holmes,' said Drew, 'but the fact is that you are beaten and the game is ours. It remains only to decide what disposal to make of you and your friends.'

'I will make you an offer,' said Holmes, coolly. 'If you will give me your word to cease your harassment of the Colonel and his family, I shall on this occasion accept it. If you then withdraw I shall not, immediately, pursue you, though I cannot guarantee that I shall not, in the fullness of time, restore all of you to your rightful places as guests of Her Majesty.'

Drew emitted a short, unpleasant laugh. 'Your eternal arrogance does not become you here, Holmes. You are in my power and have no offers to make. You have interfered once too often with matters that do not concern you and I shall have the pleasure of putting an end to the career of the greatest self-appointed meddler in the world. Numbers of my ex-colleagues at the Yard would congratulate me if they knew.'

'You and I, Drew,' said Holmes, 'have old business between us and I can understand your wish to deal with me, but is it not hard on Watson and Colonel Harden that they should die to satisfy your grudge against me?'

'If I had ever been a fair-minded man your pleas might avail,' replied Drew, 'but the stakes are too high. For all your cunning, I doubt if you understand what lies hidden in that bundle. Once it is mine and you are gone there will be no obstacle to my plans, the less so since I shall leave no loose ends.'

'Dear me,' said Holmes. 'If you will not spare my friends, at least permit an habitual smoker the courtesy of the execution yard and a last cigarette.'

Drew laughed again. 'Always the actor, Holmes,' he exclaimed, 'but your play for time will achieve nothing. These hills are empty and you have no hope of rescue. If you move I shall shoot you down in any case. You may take your cigarette, but do so slowly and carefully.'

As Holmes took his cigarette-case from his pocket I weighed up our situation, cursing the carelessness that had left both our pistols in the pockets of our coats, now draped over two distant stones, and I saw that our lantern was too far away to reach before Drew could fire.

Harden, Holmes and I each took a cigarette, and Holmes struck one of my matches. I took the last light and could not resist a poor joke.

'They used to say in Afghanistan', I remarked, 'that the third light was unlucky, for it brought the sniper's bullet, but I don't suppose that matters very much here.'

Holmes chuckled softly. 'Who knows?' he said. 'Who knows? After all, Watson, it is Midsummer's Eve and you should not be surprised at anything.'

More than once I have had occasion to watch Sherlock Holmes facing death, and it has always been with great coolness and unconcern, but now his whimsicality suggested to me that he still believed himself to be master of the situation, and I wondered what he was planning.

The darkness around us was complete and only the soughing of the night breeze in the coarse grass broke the silence as we smoked our cigarettes. About us the eternally patient stones waited for more blood. Again I sought for some chance of escape, or at least of diversion, but I saw none. Drew was right; outside the circle of the lantern's light there was nothing.

Then, distinct from the gusting of the breeze, a new sound began. I could not place its origin, for it seemed to begin softly all around us and to mount in volume. It was an eerie throbbing noise that reverberated from every direction at once and shook the air all about.

'What is that?' asked Clive, sharply, and his restless eyes shifted even faster from side to side. Malcolm, too, began to glance about him, but Drew never so much as altered his expression.

'That,' said Drew, 'is some mechanical trickery of Mr Sherlock Holmes' devising, but it will not suffice to save him.'

Hardly had he spoken the words than a spark of light flared in the brush behind him and, with a sound like tearing linen, an arc of flame ran through the dry grass.

Clive and Malcolm gasped and stepped closer to their leader, both of them casting fearful glances about them. It might be imagined that the flame in the summer-dried grass would have spread widely, but in seconds it completed a perfect circle on the slope, embracing only the two stone rings and our group, frozen between them.

'Keep your places!' Drew snapped to his henchmen. 'And keep your pistols steady! You were always a theatrical trickster, Holmes. You were a great loss to the stage and will now become a great loss to the art of detection.'

Silhouetted against the ring of fire, he raised his pistol and aimed at Holmes. My friend flung away his cigarette end and looked coolly into the pistol's barrel, his long face and magnificent eyes bright in the flickering orange light.

'We have finished our cigarettes,' he said. 'You may fire at will.'

The clank of metal sounded from beyond the circle of flames and, for the first time, Drew's eyes betrayed his unease, but still he stood and levelled his weapon.

'Look!' screeched Clive, and pointed up the dark slope dotted with the boulders of burial chambers.

A figure was moving towards the flames – the figure of a man of gigantic proportions, clad from head to foot in golden armour.

'God help us!' said Malcolm. 'What is that creature?'

Now, at last, Drew turned his head a fraction. It was enough for Sherlock Holmes. I heard a faint click and saw a flaming golden streak in the air as the blade of Holmes' sword-stick was released and he lunged at Drew. A shot flew harmlessly past him and his blade found its mark in Drew's shoulder. Cursing, Drew stumbled and sprawled to the ground, his revolver spinning from his hand.

Colonel Harden and I had both nerved ourselves to attack Drew's supporters, but it was unnecessary. Malcolm and Clive fled howling into the darkness as the awesome golden figure advanced through the wall of flame. Now my fantastic imaginings and forebodings came to life as black shapes manifested from the very ground, slid from the surrounding brush and detached themselves from the hunkered stones, leaping away into the darkness after Drew's fleeing henchmen.

Utterly unable to grasp the meaning of the events I was witnessing I turned back towards Holmes. He was wrestling with Drew, who had somehow contrived to recover his pistol. Before I could go to my friend's assistance, a shot rang out and the armoured figure staggered in its stride towards us as Drew's bullet found a mark in its helmeted head.

There was another quick glint of gold in the firelight and Drew fell still. Holmes picked himself up and drew the stained blade of his sword-stick through a handkerchief before returning it to its sheath. The huge mailed figure flung up one armoured glove and lifted its visor to reveal that there was no head within the great helmet.

'It worked, Mr Holmes, just the way you said it would,' said the muffled voice of Jay Harden, from somewhere within the resplendent armour. 'Can I get out of this suit now?'

SHERLOCK HOLMES EXPLAINS

'Well, Mr Holmes,' said the Colonel, 'I have come to realise that you don't care very much for explaining how you get your results, but if your clients have any say in the matter I'd be grateful if you'd explain a thing or two.'

We were seated around the table in the Williams' cottage, but there were no longer just the three of us. Not only was Jay Harden with us, but every chair in the house had been pressed into service to seat a half-dozen of the youths that Holmes called his 'Baker Street Irregulars', a corps of cockney street-urchins that he had maintained and trained for years and whose sharp eyes, ears and wits were often deployed in his metropolitan enquiries. Clothed now, not in their customary rags and cast-offs, but in uniform jerseys and trousers of plain black, they crowded at one end of the table, their sharp eyes gleaming from black masks where their faces had been smeared with soot. They were unusually quiet, but that was largely because they were paying earnest attention to a large cold supper and a jug of ale.

Holmes smiled across the table at Harden. 'Perhaps', he said, 'I should clarify some of my deductions in this matter.'

He poured himself a brandy and drew a crumpled map from his pocket, spreading it among the plates on the table.

'Here,' he said, pointing with a long finger, 'is a plan of this district, and it explains almost everything.'

We craned to examine the map and I could see that it was, indeed, a map of the Prescelly hills. In many places there were antiquities marked in Old English type; I saw Pentre Evan, the splendid burial monument where we had lunched on the previous day, Bedd Arthur where Holmes had set his lantern marker and Gors Fawr where we had encountered a solitary ring of small stones on a dreary moor, but none of it made any explanation that I understood.

Holmes looked up into our puzzled faces. 'I told you,' he said, 'that I had begun to doubt our original reading of the Glastonbury directions, in particular the expression "hanging stone". I had always, as you know, wondered at the message being in English and speculated as to whether that was, in itself, a clue. In addition, though I lacked the Colonel's knowledge of the musical habits of Pennsylvanian geology, I believed that I had come across the name "Ringing Stone" as a place-name somewhere in Britain. I was pursuing these questions without, I admit, any success, when serendipity laid the correct answer before my eyes.'

He paused and sipped his drink. 'Watson,' he said, 'who is himself a model of organisation and tidiness, has expostulated privately and expatiated publicly on my untidy habits but it must be said that, without them, we might never have reached our goal.'

'How come?' I enquired.

'Because, Watson, if I made a practice of neatly refolding maps after I had used them, I should not, while seeking a map of Herefordshire, have come across this sheet, folded so carelessly that I could see the name "Ringing Stone" writ large across it.'

We looked again, and again we could see no such name.

'There,' said Holmes, and laid a finger on the name of a parish. 'Maenclochog,' he read, 'or in English, Ringing Stone.'

'Then the clues are in Welsh?' said Colonel Harden.

'The essential ones,' said Holmes, 'and they were written in English precisely because they would have revealed themselves immediately in Welsh. They are all place-names.'

He moved his hand over the map. 'Here is the parish of the Ringing Stone, here is Gors Fawr – the stone circle that stands in a great waste – and here are three circles, one containing a well and one containing a grave from which the place is named – Eithbed, the Gorse Grave.'

He sat back, triumphantly, while we gazed at the sheet. 'But Holmes,' I said, 'the directions referred to the grave of Arthur's son and you told us that the cairn where you placed your lantern was Bedd Arthur – the grave of Arthur, not of his son.'

'Once I had confirmed the Gorse Grave, the great waste and the three rings,' said Holmes, 'I knew that I had discovered the correct area. It was beyond all bounds of probability that three such names should exist in any other part of Britain. It remained only to locate a grave that could be that of Arthur's son.'

Jay had sat silent, forgetting even to eat as Holmes revealed the clues, but now he frowned and spoke.

'But you read that piece from Nennius, about Arthur killing Amr and burying him by the spring at Ercing in the mound that changed shape, and you said Ercing was in Herefordshire.'

'So I did,' agreed Holmes, 'but I also told you that Arthur was credited with a great many sons. His son Llachau the Bright One is said by some to be buried somewhere on the Welsh border. While Nennius records the only report of such a grave, I reasoned that there must be another that has been forgotten and which lies in this area. I believed I had found it when I remarked this name on the map,' and he pointed again.

'The Sons of Arthur!' exclaimed the Colonel. 'What does it mean, Mr Holmes?'

'Merely', said Holmes, 'that the valley contains two solitary stones that locals call the Sons of Arthur.'

'Then why did you reject it?' I asked.

'Because it is a valley,' replied Holmes. 'Neither of the stones could possibly be seen from the Gorse Grave at Eithbed, whereas I was seeking a grave on a height. Now this ridge is covered in burial cairns, as you have seen, but Arthur's Sons gave me an indication.'

'How so?' said Harden.

'The name exists because one or more of Arthur's sons are supposed to have died in that valley. If that is so, then he or they would have been buried nearby, and there,' he stabbed at the map, 'is a cairn on the highest point of the ridge, immediately above the valley, a cairn called Bedd Arthur. We know it was not Arthur's grave. What else can it be but a misremembered grave of a son of King Arthur?'

He took out his cherrywood pipe and lit it, while we absorbed his reasoning.

'I do not believe,' said the Colonel after a moment, 'that there is another man in the world who could have unravelled this and reasoned it all out so skilfully.'

'Tush, Colonel, I freely admit that I virtually forced my services upon you in the first place when none of us had any idea of the real nature of the mystery. It was purely fortuitous that you engaged an agent who has made special studies both of ancient ciphers and of the Celtic languages.'

I had a suspicion that he was about to change the subject, and there was much more that I needed to hear.

'But Drew,' I said. 'How did he get on our track?'

'Now there,' said Holmes, 'I must plead guilty. I had pointed out to you, Colonel, that Drew must be dealt with if you and your family were to be safe, and so I took precautions to ensure that he would learn of our whereabouts. I informed the United States Embassy in London and the Consulates at Swansea and Milford Haven of your presence in this vicinity, under the excuse of concern for your safety. I had little doubt that the information would speedily reach Drew and, indeed, he was behind us in less than twenty-four hours.'

I recalled his watchfulness during our first day among the hills and realised he had been looking for confirmation that we were being followed.

'But what about Jay and his new friends?' asked the Colonel.

'Despite your willingness to act as bait for Drew,' said Holmes, 'I felt we needed some additional protection and the possibilities of diversions. The official police would have kept Drew away, as would an obvious bodyguard. You will recall that he made no move at Glastonbury while we were accompanied by McMurdo's men. I felt that cunning and surprise were perhaps more valuable to us than strength, so I called upon my faithful Irregulars and provided them with a few surprises.'

Harden shook his head and looked at his son. 'And Jay? How did he get into the act?'

'I plead guilty again,' said Holmes. 'It was entirely my idea and he was unwilling to take part without your permission, which I could not allow him to seek. I was driven to persuade him by introducing him to Henry Irving in his dressing-room. I assumed, rightly it seems, that Drew would be content to let us find his quarry then seek to take it from us and eliminate us. At that point I wanted Drew and his devil-haunted friends to be severely startled, and that meant startling you and Watson as well.'

'Well, you certainly succeeded there,' said Harden. 'How was it all done?'

'The fire was simply a matter of chemicals in the grass. Once they were alight I knew that the arrival of Jay in a suit of theatrical armour borrowed from my friend Irving would have a salutary effect on the over-stretched nerves of our opponents.'

'But Jay was nearly shot!' I protested.

'Not so nearly,' said Holmes. 'Irving's armour is virtually full weight, to provide a realistic clanking sound. I doubt that a pistol bullet would have penetrated very far. Only the head-piece is a light shell and that, as you saw, was empty. I believe it has figured in the first act of *Hamlet*.'

'What on earth was that strange sound that filled the air?' I asked.

'Really,' said my friend, 'I thought that with your Antipodean experiences you might have recognised it.' He motioned to the Irregulars and one of them took something from his pocket and passed it across. It was two pieces of polished hardwood connected by a length of cord.

'I have never seen one before,' I admitted. 'What is it?'

'A ritual device of the Wonghibbon tribe of New South Wales, I believe,' said Holmes. 'It is called a bull-roarer and is used to dismay the enemy.'

We laughed, but Jay looked suddenly serious. 'Will there be any – any trouble over Drew?' he asked, hesitantly. Holmes' second blow with the sword-stick had finished the renegade detective and his remains now filled the pit we had excavated.

'I should doubt it,' said Holmes. 'Clive and Malcolm may have escaped the Irregulars, but they have no reason to publicise this affair and, were they to do so, I should expect to be acquitted. No, they will slink back to their usual haunts and continue to avoid the law.'

'Will you go after them?' asked Harden. 'Not if they give me no further reason,' said Holmes. 'Drew was the serpent's head and we have crushed it. I have completed a piece of work I began many years ago and fulfilled my obligations to you, Colonel.'

'Oh, you have done that very completely,' said Harden, 'but there remains one important question.'

'What is that?' said Holmes.

'What the blazes is inside that bundle we hauled out of the pit?'

'Ha!' ejaculated Holmes. 'I had become so busy congratulating myself on having scotched the last of Moriarty's poisonous empire that I had forgotten that little problem. What do you imagine we have found, gentlemen?'

'I haven't the least idea,' said the Colonel. 'I have racked my brains to figure out what could drive men like Moriarty and Drew to such lengths, but I have no answer.'

'If it is what I fear,' said Holmes, 'then it is better left till morning.' He rose and stretched himself. 'The Irregulars must get back to their camp and we must have some rest. Leave me to investigate our trophy and tomorrow we shall see what we have.'

27

THE DEVIL'S GRAIL

I cannot speak for the Hardens, but I suspect that the end of our exertions let them sleep as deeply and dreamlessly as did I. It was later rather than sooner when I woke next morning, to find the water cooling in my shaving jug and the scent of breakfast rising up the stairs. With wakefulness, my curiosity returned with a rush and I made a hasty toilet and presented myself downstairs to learn when Holmes would reveal the last element in our extraordinary adventures.

The Hardens, father and son, were before me at table and I greeted them. 'Good morning,' I said. 'Is Holmes not up yet?'

'Mrs Williams says that Mr Holmes is in the garden and will we be so kind as to join him when we have breakfasted,' said Jay, passing the toast rack.

'He is not usually an early riser,' I remarked.

'Is he not?' asked Jay. 'Well, he came to meet me and the Irregulars just after dawn two days ago, to make sure that all the arrangements would work.'

I laughed ruefully as I recalled the morning when Holmes convinced the Colonel and me that he had developed a healthy interest in a morning walk. Harden chuckled too.

'You have a pretty unique partner, doctor,' he said. 'How do you manage with him?'

'I suppose,' I replied, 'that it is because our mental processes are so entirely dissimilar that I never get in his way.'

'You do yourself too little justice,' said the Colonel. 'It is very evident to me that Sherlock Holmes values your collaboration and, after our adventures at Wormlow, I have some idea why.'

I was pleased to hear him say so, but he went on.

'To tell you the truth, doctor, I'm glad of the chance of a quiet word with you. Now that this affair is almost over there is the question of Mr Holmes' fees. What do you think is fitting?'

'Oh, I have no influence whatsoever over his professional charges,' I said. 'He told you at Winchester that his rates never vary unless he decides to remit them entirely, and I believe that to be true.'

Harden shook his head. 'He has removed a threat from my family, rescued my son twice and saved my own life. Into the bargain he has shown me the most exciting times I've had since they signed the peace at Appomattox. I guess that's worth quite a lot.'

Breakfast over, we took our coffee and strolled out into the cottage garden. It was a perfect midsummer morning and the air was ripe with the scent of the flowers that framed a small patch of lawn. A tang of smoke reached us and I thought it to be from Holmes' meerschaum, but it came from a small fire that smouldered between the flower-beds, near to where Holmes sat at a rustic table. A pot of coffee steamed on the table and behind him the green slopes of the hills were bright under the sun, giving no hint of their dark and ancient secrets.

He raised a hand in greeting and waved us to seats at a bench opposite to him. As we sat I could see from his pallor and the shadows under his eyes that he had not slept.

'You have been up all night,' I accused him.

'True, Watson,' he said, and pointed to a wooden box that lay on the table beside him. 'I have passed the night in learning what it is that we uncovered.'

We looked at the plain box of dark wood, some two feet long by a foot and a half wide and maybe eight or nine inches deep. It was undecorated except for its hinges and fastenings, which were of silver and evidently of very ancient manufacture.

'And what might it be?' I asked.

'I had formed some opinions when I sought information in the British Museum,' he said. 'The records of King Henry's Commissioners referred to their search for what they called "the black missal" and once it was called a "treatise". I believed that we might be looking for one of those ancient grimoires, textbooks of magic created in the Middle Ages. They are much sought after by deviants like Drew and by the curious and gullible, and the prices that they attract have led to the institution of a manufactory at Venice that churns out poor forgeries for the dealers of Rome, Paris and London. I thought that we might have enriched our national collections with a rare and genuine example. Nevertheless, I could not understand the obsessive interest of Moriarty and Drew, let alone King Henry.'

He paused and refreshed his coffee while we waited expectantly. 'But you have found something else, I reckon,' said the Colonel.

'So I have,' said Holmes. 'Something so unique that I could never have guessed at its existence and so corrupt that I devoutly wish I had remained in ignorance of it.'

He unfastened the silver clasps of the box and raised its lid. Inside lay a rectangular object wrapped in white chamois leather. Holmes drew it out and unwrapped it, laying it on the table.

As the rays of the sun struck it a blaze of colours lit and shimmered before our eyes. Before we knew what it was that we saw we had gasped at the burning beauty of it. After a moment I could see that we were looking at a richly enamelled cover, decorated with the fantastic patterns of a bygone age and set with jewelled ornaments at many points. Though it had been sealed in darkness for centuries, its tints were as vivid as though they had been painted that morning.

Young Jay exclaimed and I gasped. Colonel Harden gave a long low sound of admiration. 'What a wonderful object!' he said. 'What is it, Mr Holmes?'

Holmes' long fingers traced the twisting, writhing patterns across the cover. 'Beneath this elaboration,' he said, 'you can, perhaps, see a pattern we have seen before – the Zodiac of thirteen houses. It is, as I surmised, a treatise from the cult of the Mother Goddess, but not quite what I suspected it to be.'

He opened the cover, revealing pages of parchment, covered with handwritten text but with their margins and initial letters decorated with the same fantastic imagery that enriched the outer covers.

'Then what is it?' I asked.

' "A great book; a great evil",' he quoted. 'For all its rich beauty it is, I think, the vilest thing that I have ever held in my hands. Let me translate its opening for you.'

He spread the pages with his hands and began to read aloud:

'We are taught by the oldest laws of our people that there is no wickedness greater than treachery; that he who betrays another, most especially he who bears false witness against another, is a serpent whose venom spatters all, and the example of Judas is held ever before us. So men have withstood torture and gone to the most fearful deaths rather than betray their fellows. Yet it should be known that, before the days of Christ, there were practices and receipts by which a man might be turned from any allegiance so that he would with great willingness tell all of his most secret knowledge and so that he would, by very little suggestion, speak against his former brothers whatsoever falsehoods might be suggested to him and much that he may imagine, for such is the worth of these things that when they are complete it may be truly said that his soul is not his own and he will speak the truths that he has held hidden in his heart or what falsehood may be laid upon his tongue. By these means may be armies betrayed and princes overthrown in secret'.

Holmes paused and looked around at us. 'So that his soul is not his own,' he repeated. 'This wretched book is a textbook for the destruction of the human brain and for the perversion of the highest attributes of mankind. The meanest gutter-thief of our lowest slum holds it his only virtue that he is loyal to his kind; the highest and best in the land hold their obligations by the giving of their oath. This filthy treatise teaches how to dissolve those bonds of loyalty and make the brains and hearts of others mere playthings of the evilly disposed.'

'That is, surely, impossible,' I said.

'Would that it were, Watson. Sadly, your profession is only just seeking the mechanisms of the brain that make men what they are and drive them to do what they do. If you could read this text you would learn that your colleagues have been forestalled by centuries. Here are regimens of drugs that destroy the memory or loosen the most closely guarded tongue; here are practices of cruelty so subtle they leave no mark upon the body but warp the mind and heart beyond recognition.'

'But who could have written it? Where does it come from?' asked Harden.

'There are two texts,' said Holmes. 'The introduction is in the Welsh of the Middle Ages and written by one who professed Christianity, but it introduces an older text in an older form of Brythonic Celtic. It may come out of the Dark Ages or even earlier. I have read the whole of it and it harrows the soul. Whatever age spawned it must have been a veritably dark age. I have passed a dismal night, gentlemen, looking into the rules of hell.'

He turned and gazed across the green hills while he drew on his pipe. The bright pages ruffled slightly in the breeze.

'Surely,' said Harden, 'most of those old grimoires are mere rigmaroles of superstitious nonsense. Isn't this the same?'

'No,' said Holmes. 'This is a practical treatise which, I am sure, would do exactly what it promises.'

'Then what will you do with it?' asked Harden.

'There is no question,' said Holmes, and he turned back to the table. He took out his pocket-knife and snapped it open, slashing it quickly across the open book to sever a page.

'Wait!' cried Harden. 'You can't do that! You are destroying a unique treasure!'

'I can do no other,' said Holmes, evenly, and he sliced away another page. 'This thing cannot be permitted to exist. As long as it does it will be the goal of evil men like Henry and Moriarty and Drew, and what use they might make of it does not bear contemplation. Judas destroyed himself in his guilt – to what Aceldama would we come if we allowed this evil to persist? I do not know what reward or punishment I may merit when I leave this world, but I am quite certain that I should deserve the lowest circle of hell if I failed to destroy this loathsome thing.'

He flung the cut pages on to the little garden fire and the flames ran quickly across the dry parchment, blackening the rich patterns. Harden half rose as though to snatch them from the flames, but then sank back upon his seat.

In silence we watched as Sherlock Holmes hacked out the twenty or so pages that the jewelled folder contained and consigned each one to the fire. The flames flared blue and green as they fed on the rich colours of the painted skin, but at last there was nothing left save a few twisted shreds of carbon writhing in the embers.

Holmes closed the rich covers, wrapped them in the chamois and placed them back in the box. He handed it to the Colonel.

'A souvenir,' he said.

'I cannot take that,' protested Harden. 'It is a national treasure. It should be in the British Museum.'

'If you do not, then it will follow its contents into the flames,' said Holmes. 'It is hardly such as I could display upon the mantelpiece at Baker Street, nor present to a national collection. How would I explain to a treasure trove jury or the Trustees of the British Museum that I chose to destroy the contents of the box?'

Harden chuckled. 'By heavens, Mr Holmes,' he said, 'I am deeply grateful to you for everything that you have done for me and mine and I should be meeting your fee, but instead you hand me a king's ransom.' He took out his pocket-book and withdrew a cheque. 'I hope,' he said, 'that this is sufficient to pay the reckoning.'

Holmes glanced only briefly at the slip before returning it to the Colonel. 'It is a great deal too much, Colonel. Deduct from it whatever reward you would give to the farm-boy who helped your son and promise me a place in your manufactories or plantations for any of my Irregulars who fancy a wider future than the alleys of London offer. Oh, and so that Watson will not regard me as dishonest, deduct also the price of your dressing-gown that was destroyed at Glastonbury.'

The Colonel smiled. 'You have my hand on it, Mr Holmes,' and he suited the action to the word.

Holmes' wan features warmed with a smile as he clasped the American's hand. Behind him the morning breeze blew away the last dark fragments of the Devil's Grail.

'EDITOR'S NOTES'

As with the previous manuscript that I have edited, *Sherlock Holmes and the railway maniac*, I have spent some time in researching aspects of the narrative that might confirm its authenticity. My researches are, I am sure, incomplete, and what follows merely records what little I have found. I would welcome any light that others may throw on any aspect of the story of the Devil's Grail.

Chapter One
The inevitable difficulty arises over the identity of Holmes' client. Watson claimed never to have exposed a client to recognition, and some or all of his details may be invented. If not, a Virginian millionaire tobacco-grower whose son became a cannery magnate ought to be traceable. Jay Harden suggests that his own son became a film actor and there is an intriguing hint later in the story that 'Wayne' was a family name; but then, John Wayne's real name was Marion Morrison.

Chapter Three
The weapon used against Holmes was certainly one that really existed. To the best of my belief they have not been manufactured since World War Two, but I could be wrong. There is at least one unsolved murder case in Britain where the weapon was believed to have been a poacher's gun.

Chapter Four

If this is an authentic Watson narrative it will settle a problem that has vexed commentators for many years. In 'The Solitary Cyclist' Watson asserts that it was Saturday, 23rd April 1895 when Violet Smith consulted Holmes, at which time the great detective was more interested in the persecution of the Harden family. He goes on to say that Miss Smith's case ended one week later, on Saturday, 30th April. Many critics have pointed out that these dates were not Saturdays and have removed the case to another year in their chronologies or suggested that he wrote 13th and 20th April in such a very medical hand that his figures were misread.

The present story makes it completely clear that, whatever day of the week it may have been, Miss Violet Smith consulted Holmes on 23rd April, her case was over on 30th April and Holmes and Watson went to Winchester in answer to Harden's summons on 1st May.

Chapter Five

We have become so accustomed to kidnapping that it seems unbelievable that, less than a century ago, the crime was virtually unknown outside the bandit-haunted areas of southern Europe. The taking of little Charlie Ross from his parents' lawn was a crime that rocked America and, as Holmes says, he was never found. There was an extensive ransom correspondence and the police found and began to track the kidnappers, hoping to find where the boy was hidden. Unluckily, the kidnappers attempted a burglary and were met with vigorously American resistance which killed them all. As late as the 1940s persons were emerging who claimed to be Charlie Ross.

Chapter Six

Buried in Jay's exciting narrative is a reference to what can only have been the great Buddy Bolden, known to some as the 'Grandfather of Jazz'. Who else was called Bolden and led an orchestra in New Orleans in the early 1890s?

Bolden's Ragtime Orchestra was a great favourite of the French community in the city, playing for balls and garden parties, and Aunt Mimi may well have known him. Colonel Harden might have been even less amused by his sister-in-law's social indiscretions if he had realised that her escort on Congo Square was a Negro ragtime trumpeter.

The French and Spanish slave-owners of the South were more liberal in their treatment of slaves and permitted them to gather on Congo Square, where they drummed and danced and recreated the rituals of their African past. The practice began long before the Civil War and only died out around the turn of the century.

Watson never expands his diagnosis that Drew suffered from a 'diseased larynx', but unless I am well wide of the mark, I believe he is discreetly telling us that Drew was syphilitic.

Chapter Seven
Wayles Court and its former owner both have invented names and, as Holmes points out, there are many such houses in Hampshire, but a check on Royal garden parties in the county against society suicides might reveal the real location.

The thirteen-house Zodiac including the sign of Ophiocus the Serpent Bearer was, and is, used by some adherents of the cult of the Mother Goddess.

Chapter Eight
It is, perhaps, possible to identify the villainous Drew from Holmes' remarks in this chapter and from later references to Drew's immediate henchmen as being another ex-detective and a former solicitor.

In 1877 Scotland Yard was wracked by scandal when it was discovered that officers at the Yard had become involved (through connections made in Masonic lodges) with two international confidence tricksters called Benson and Kurr. These two wrote to wealthy and sporting men and women, claiming to be racing tipsters who were so successful that no bookie would accept their bets. They invited their victims to place bets for them on a commission basis. If the proposition was accepted, they supplied cheques, details of bets and the name of the bookie with whom the bet should be placed. Initially the bets would succeed and the agent would receive the commission due. Inevitably, the agents would, eventually, place a large bet of their own alongside one of Benson's, at which point the bookie would vanish with their money, having been a part of Benson's gang.

Chief Inspector Druscovitch, a naturalised Pole, got into financial difficulties and confided in a colleague, Chief Inspector Meiklejohn. Meiklejohn, who was already in the clutches of Kurr, arranged for Druscovitch to be lent £60 in return for a tip-off if the Yard intended to arrest Benson and Kurr.

When, at last, the Yard became suspicious, it was Druscovitch who was ordered to act against the gang and he earned 'rewards' of hundreds of pounds by suppressing telegrams from other forces and tipping off Kurr as to impending arrests. He was, at length, sent to Rotterdam to arrest Benson and could not do otherwise, but his days were numbered. When Benson and his confederates were convicted they told the police of their corrupt connections with Scotland Yard. Druscovitch, Meiklejohn, a Chief Inspector called Palmer and a dishonest solicitor called Froggatt were tried and sentenced to two years' hard labour, the maximum sentence. Another Chief Inspector, Clarke, was acquitted and retired early.

Palmer became a publican and Meiklejohn a private enquiry agent; Froggatt died in a workhouse, but nothing is known of Druscovitch's movements after his release from prison. It seems likely to me that Watson has disguised Druscovitch as 'Drew' and Meiklejohn and Froggatt as the 'Malcolm' and 'Clive' who appear later in the narrative, perhaps reducing their erstwhile rank as a sop to the wounded feelings of friends at the Yard. It would explain why Druscovitch disappeared from history.

Colonel Harden's reference to Fort Sumter is to the place where the first shots of the American Civil War were fired, and he is correct that General Robert E. Lee, another Virginian, when offered the command of the Union armies told Lincoln that, if Virginia seceded from the Union, he would follow his native State, 'with my sword and, if need be, with my life'. He accepted the Confederate command and so became probably the only soldier in history to be given the personal choice of commanding the winners or the losers.

Chapter Nine
The retired prize-fighter McMurdo was, literally, an old sparring partner of Holmes, who makes his first appearance in 'The Sign of Four'.

A 'red kettle' was cockney for a gold watch, as a 'white kettle' was a silver watch. The terms still survive among the older market grafters, but few recognise that they are rhyming slang, 'kettle and hob' rhyming with 'watch and fob'.

Chapter Ten
Freddy Porlock appears in a passing reference in 'The Valley of Fear' as Holmes' contact inside Moriarty's organisation, but without detail. It is interesting to have a clearer portrait of him

The Abbé Boudet and his strange book and the British Israelites are all real; indeed the latter still publish their bizarre theories. It is beyond argument that Holmes, with his profound scholarship in ancient languages and the history of the Celts, would have had no time for such theories.

Chapter Eleven
The splendid clock at Wells is not, of course, Watson's invention, but the invention of a Glastonbury monk, six hundred years ago. It still tells the time and performs its astonishing party piece.

Chapter Twelve
Glastonbury Abbey does lay claim to be the resting place of Saints David, Patrick, Brigid and Dunstan as well as

King Arthur. Irish readers will, naturally, continue to believe that Patrick is buried at one of three places in Ireland, but he may well have ended his days at Glastonbury and been buried there.

At the time of the present narrative, in midsummer of 1895, the site of the abbey would have been the wilderness that Watson describes. It had been derelict since 1539 and was used as a convenient supply of cut building stones. It was not purchased by the Church of England until 1908.

Tourists who might wish to follow Holmes' travels, and hoteliers who might wish to erect 'Sherlock Holmes slept here' plaques, are endlessly frustrated by Watson's use of false names for hotels, but here he gives away a clue by referring to the four-poster beds at their hotel. It seems extremely likely that they stayed in Glastonbury's famous George and Pilgrims in the High Street which, I believe, can still supply four-poster beds.

Chapter Fourteen
Almost as great a mystery as the Glastonbury fragment itself is the question of Colonel Harden's experimental camera. It is true that archaeologists and other analysts now use computer enhancement for exactly the purposes Harden envisaged, and that does allow the recovery of faint inscriptions, but it seems highly improbable that the same effect could have been obtained by any application of stereoscopy. The Colonel admitted that adjustments of his device were highly sensitive. Was he, perhaps, misled by some accidental effect that could not be systematised, and is that the reason why his device has been forgotten by history?

The passage from William of Malmesbury is accurate and no editor that I have come across has ever sought to explain it in detail.

Chapter Fifteen
That the mantelpiece clock at Baker Street was unreliable is, I believe, established by one of Paget's original illustrations which shows it to be seriously wrong.

Chapter Sixteen

It may be that it was the Glastonbury case that finally persuaded Holmes to commit to paper his knowledge of codes and ciphers; W.S. Baring-Gould, in his *Sherlock Holmes: a Biography of the World's First Consulting Detective* (Hart Davis 1962, Panther 1975), lists a publication by Holmes called *Secret Writings*, privately published in London in the year after this case. Unhappily, no copy is now known to exist. Those who discount Holmes' claims to knowledge of many ancient languages should remember that Baring-Gould's bibliography also lists another publication by Holmes: *A Study of the Chaldean Roots in the Ancient Cornish Language*, published by Keun and Sons three years later.

Chapter Nineteen

In my researches into this chapter I must acknowledge the considerable assistance of Mr Patrick McSweeney and the staffs of the Hereford and Ross-on-Wye public libraries. They helped me to check Watson's information about the 'Tump' at Wormlow (now spelt Wormelow). They also unearthed for me a copy of the minutes of Herefordshire's Woolhope Club for the Annual General Meeting in 1928, where it is recorded that Wormelow Tump had been removed some years earlier in order to widen the road.

Speaking of the Woolhope Club, perhaps its best remembered luminary was Alfred Watkins who, in 1925, published *The Old Straight Track* (republished Garnstone Press, 1970) in which he revealed his theories about what he called 'ley lines' in the landscape. Was he, by any chance, the member of the club that Watson and the Colonel met in the library at Ross-on-Wye?

Chapter Twenty-one

'Macing the rattler' was underworld slang for travelling on the railway without a ticket, 'rattler' being a train and 'mace' meaning 'to rob or fiddle', a sense which it still retains.

187

Chapter Twenty-two

It is, maybe, impossible to establish the authenticity of the Watson manuscript beyond any doubt; one can only accumulate evidence and make one's own decision as to where the balance lies. Nevertheless, a strong point in favour of its authenticity emerges from Colonel Harden's reminiscence about the ringing rocks, for it turns out to be true that, in 1890, a Dr Ott appeared at a meeting of the Buck Wampum Literary and Historical Association of Ottsville, Pennsylvania and played tunes on pieces of ringing rock, accompanied by the Pleasant Valley Band! He was not, in fact, the first in his field, for a few years earlier my home town of Walsall had witnessed a performance by a band that played on rocks, though whether of British or Pennsylvanian origin I have been unable to discover. They advertised themselves as 'The Rock Band'.

Chapter Twenty-three

The handsome monument with a striking view is, of course, the remains of a chambered tomb now known as Pentre Ifan, though a century ago it was known as Pentre Evan. Visitors often believe that Ifan or Evan was the name of the individual who merited this splendid tomb. Unfortunately it is merely the name of a former owner of the farm on whose land the monument stands.

Chapter Twenty-four

Perhaps the saddest description in Watson's story is of the triple circle at Eithbed. There are few such complexes in Britain (there is one at Avebury and another at Stanton Drew) and, I believe, no other megalithic ring with a living spring at its centre, but one would seek in vain for the remains that Watson describes.

In the *Archaeologia Cambrensis* of July 1911, the Reverend W. Done Bushell described his researches among the Prescelly monuments. He was a disciple of Lockyer, who first discovered that ancient monuments often incorporated astronomical alignments, and so he surveyed and planned the circles with care and left us a detailed plan of the Eithbed complex. His plan is, alas, all that remains of the Eithbed site, which is now completely bare. Bushell explained in his paper that the stones had:

> ... only sixteen months before, that is to say in the summer of 1909, been broken up, and carried off to build an ugly house which stands close by, a veritable monument of shame. However, the destroyer probably did not know what he was doing. A relative of his, who was present when the deed was done, and who himself assisted at the demolition, told me without reserve exactly what had taken place, nor did it seem to him that there was anything demanding much apology; but it remains that thus before our very eyes these interesting vestiges of prehistoric man have, like so many others, perished out of the land.

The Gorse Grave was opened in 1910, to reveal a stone chamber containing a quantity of organic ash.

Chapter Twenty-six
Despite the fate of the Eithbed circles, the Sons of Arthur still stand, as does Bedd Arthur and the little circle at Gors Fawr, but a complex of circles and an avenue which lay near the Sons of Arthur have been destroyed.

The passing reference to Irving only increases one's desire to identify the Harden family. Did John Vincent junior, who, in his youth, knew Buddy Bolden, Sherlock Holmes and Henry Irving, leave no memoirs?

We never discover how Clive and Malcolm succeeded in escaping the Baker Street Irregulars, but the answer is probably a combination of blind terror and a convenient vehicle.

Chapter Twenty-seven
Speculation as to the origin of the Devil's Grail is probably fruitless. The Druids, priests of the Celts, were widely

learned but never recorded anything in writing and, in any case, held beliefs that would seem to have excluded the practices detailed in the book. During the Dark Ages, the Anglo-Saxon invaders introduced a number of regrettable practices into Britain, including cannibalism, but they, of course, did not write in Welsh.

I have cited any points which I believe may throw light on the manuscript. Personally I am satisfied that we have here another of Watson's unpublished records, but readers must reach their own decisions.

Barrie Roberts